T0149184

THROUGH
MY EYES

HUMOR & TRAGEDY OF
LAW ENFORCEMENT

JON STANLEY

authorHOUSE®

AuthorHouse™
1663 Liberty Drive
Bloomington, IN 47403
www.authorhouse.com
Phone: 1 (800) 839-8640

Published by AuthorHouse 10/24/2016

ISBN: 978-1-5246-4595-3 (sc)
ISBN: 978-1-5246-4594-6 (e)

Library of Congress Control Number: 2016917339

Print information available on the last page.

Contents

BOOK DEDICATION

Ronald Edward Stanley, Dad - Retired with 41 years in Law Enforcement in the State of Florida. Assistant Chief of Police, Dade City, FL; Major at Alachua County Sheriff's Department in charge of the Criminal Investigation Division, also held positions of Director of Region II Investigations, and Inspector - Bureau of Operations, Gainesville, FL; Director of the National Intelligence Academy, Ft. Lauderdale, FL; Chief Deputy, Bureau of Operations & Chief Criminal Investigator, Pasco County Sheriff's Department, Dade City, FL; Chief Deputy Bureau of Operations, Polk County Sheriff's Office, Bartow, FL; Crime Prevention Specialist, Florida Farm Bureau, Gainesville, FL; Financial Investigator Supervisor, State of Florida, Office of Comptroller, Tampa, FL

Jessie Edward Stanley, Grandfather- Deceased - Served as elected Constable in Pasco County Florida, 1943-1965. The Constable was a constitutional law enforcement officer through the Executive Department, State of Florida.

Gene "Jimmy" Terry, Friend and ex-partner – Rose through the ranks from Deputy Sheriff to Chief Deputy and is now retired from the Sumter County Sheriff's Department, Bushnell, FL

Raymond R. More, Grandfather - Deceased - Police Officer, Dade City, Florida

Colleen B. Stanley, Wife - 15 years as Law Enforcement Officer - Coleman Police Department, Coleman, Florida; Wildwood Police Department, Wildwood, Florida; Leesburg Police Department, Leesburg, Florida; and Florida State University Police Department, Tallahassee, Florida. Her experience includes patrol, investigations, K-9 officer, bicycle patrol, worked with narcotics task force, and crisis intervention unit. Prior to becoming a LEO, she worked in records at Belle Glade Police Department and as a police dispatcher at Palm Beach County Sheriff's Office, Belle Glade, FL, and Lake County Sheriff's Office, Tavares, FL.

John VonKossovsky, Friend - Retired in 2008 from the Broward County Sheriff's Department, Ft. Lauderdale, Florida. John was a fellow officer at Belle Glade Police Department, Belle Glade, FL. I trained John when he first became an officer in 1978. I first met John in 1974 while I was a deputy with the Palm Beach County Sheriff's Office. We continue to be friends to this day.

Through My Eyes

From the Author

While growing up my two grandfathers, Jessie Edward Stanley and Raymond More, as well as my father, Ronald Edward Stanley was in law enforcement. I truly began to think that one day I might want to become a law enforcement officer. During those early years, especially while attending high school, I always wondered what it would be like to strap on a gun, pin on a badge and become a LAWMAN. However, there were many questions running through my mind. Many of these questions were answered over the next few years while finishing high school and serving in the U.S. Army. Now let's discuss the police image and the police officer.

The Police Image - What can and should be done about it? Is there a problem? Yes, a very definite problem, particularity in our cities. Some of the causes and some of the remedies are clear, however, the problem is a deep and complex one involving many areas; some of which are outside the police control.

First and perhaps foremost there has been a very definite social change in the United States in the last fifty years. To a large extent the public has refused to recognize this change and the police as a whole have not bothered to understand the justification and in some cases lack of justification in this social change. The public has attempted and in some cases used the police to fight some of the social changes.

The very nature of law enforcement places a very heavy burden on the police officer as far as his image is concerned. There is no possible way for the police officer to enforce the law and preserve the peace without creating some ill feelings. For example, traffic enforcement; most individuals resent an officer stopping him or her for a traffic violation and the fact that he or she was violating the law makes the person all the more resentful. No individual likes for his movements to be restricted for any reason. Traffic should be an area of great concern for the progressive law enforcement official.

The charges of "Police Brutality" have had a very damaging effect on the police image over the years. We in law enforcement would be less than truthful if we did not admit that the use of excessive force has been a problem in the United States for years and still exists to a large degree today. However, I do not believe it is anywhere near the problem today as some people would have society as a whole to believe. But the truth remains that we can ill afford to have it exist in any degree. In my opinion, the problem of the use of excessive force is nowhere near as prevalent as verbal abuse and harassment.

Civil disobedience and civil rights demonstration have certainly cast a shadow over the police image over the past fifty to sixty years. Many of the demonstrations are in defiance of the law in an effort to force recourse in our courts. This of course means violations of the law, the law we are sworn to uphold as law enforcement officers. In the performance of our duty, we are often blamed for the original cause and issues. We are caught up in the web of problems confronting society today. Despite the fact that many of our law enforcement agencies make every effort to handle these situations fairly and professionally, they are still condemned and accused of countless acts of brutality. Often we must act because our government officials and judicial officials have failed to live up to their responsibilities. This brings us to another problem; that of community accountability.

It has often been said that you can judge a community by its police department. I think what is meant by this is the fact that a majority of law enforcement agencies reflect the attitude of the community. This is justifiable and proper as long as the community is demanding good law enforcement and is prepared to pay for this service. However, when a community refuses to live up to its responsibilities in these areas, including social changes, then the responsible police administrator should see that his department is a professionalized force capable of setting an example for all the citizens to follow.

What of our recent Supreme Court decisions? Here again the police are often blamed when a dangerous criminal is released on society. The public often only hears that the defendant was released because evidence obtained by police officers was inadmissible. They assume the police officer made a mistake, not realizing that the evidence was gathered and presented in compliance with existing procedures only to have the Supreme Court rule on some newly presented question concerning one of the amendments to the constitution. The police image goes down one more notch and often through no fault of the police. This brings us to the question, what can and must be done to improve the police image?

I have serious reservations concerning a separate police community relations unit. In my opinion, police community relations are not merely a problem of a special police unit. The public tends to see the police as a group, consequently, when a single or small number of police officers are abusive in their everyday contacts with the public the department as a whole suffers.

The problem that exists between the police and the community is not merely because of lack of communications or information, and it will not be solved by having a special unit educate the community, concerning their activities. Instead the conflict concerns real points of disagreements "how the police treat citizens on the street", "how citizens' complaints are handled", etc.

If we are to deal effectively with our problems with the minority groups and other citizens, then we must adopt a professional approach toward community relations. These problems must be confronted frankly and openly. We must improve our procedure for handling citizens' complaints, we must maintain professional selection in our recruitment, local government must be willing to accept their responsibility, the community must be willing to have its laws enforced without discrimination, the public must withhold criticism of the police until the facts are known, and then criticize or support the police responsible. The minorities must be willing to accept their responsibility and to aid the police when necessary. With all of this, the primary responsibility still rests with the police. We must take the initiative in bringing about good police/community relations. We must remember that the majority of American's respect their police force, but we must also face the fact that the very people who need police protection the most; the poor and the minority groups, often fear and distrust the police. Strict adherence to plain old everyday courtesy and common sense would help.

When we talk of the police image, we of course look at the individual officer. When we think of the individual we must realize that he/she is a human being with attitudes, biases, and prejudice. The public on the other hand sees him/her as a symbol of law and order and only looks at his/her behavior. To compound matters, they look at his/her behavior 24 hours a day. What then, is the answer?

If we accept the fact that behavior is a learned process, then we must accept the fact that education is in part the answer. We find many of our top officials are self-educated men albeit very competent police officials. But I must agree with several experts on the subject. This type of administrator has no place in our society of today or tomorrow. In my opinion, most of the self-educated police officials have kept abreast of the rapid changes in law enforcement and are intelligent, dedicated, police professionals. However, the pressing problem today is the need for intelligent and dedicated recruits, regardless of formal education.

The public will demand higher standards as police officers obtain higher pay. Faced with this justifiable fact we must be professional in our selection, recruit training, in service training, special training, and our command personnel training. We in law enforcement must realize that the higher paid, better qualified recruits will not come about overnight. The problem has been with us for a number of years and we have made great strides in remedying it. We must continue with the concerted effort toward these goals.

We must not let education blind us to the fact that recruit training and in service training must be geared to teach human relations and understanding of the basic needs and desires of all humans, especially those that require most of our service. The formal education of a recruit is not the last answer. Many of these people have had little or no experience or exposure to the poor or minority groups. Not having this, they would find it extremely difficult to deal with these people; however, they should be better prepared to acquire this understanding.

Lack of recruitment from the minority groups should not be blamed entirely on law enforcement. The communities themselves must share the responsibility. They are largely responsible for this condition. Even the minority groups themselves have prevented this recruitment. I must stress the fact that lowering of the standards should not occur in order to recruit from the minority groups. It would be unfair to the community, to the department, and to the recruit.

The sum of the entire problem, in my opinion, lies in the fact that the police image results from or at least is greatly influenced by the action of the individual officer in his everyday contact with the public on the street. While the police/community relations units and other similar units may help, they will have little lasting effect if the public is not treated properly on a day to day, person to person basis.

It must be remembered that if the officer is not well qualified or if he has not been properly trained, or if he is prejudice, then his anger and resentment may overcome his better judgment.

It must also be remembered that in order for law enforcement officers to advance toward better justice we must begin with a greater knowledge of the law. Respect for the law, which is a prerequisite of law observance, can hardly be expected of people in general if we as officers do not set the example of obedience to its precepts.

What better image can we have then that of a physically fit, well dressed, courteous, intelligent, and knowledgeable officer treating everyone fairly and impartially with a keen sense of justice and dedication to society and his profession.

It's now been many years since I retired from Law Enforcement. Like Paul Harvey used to say, "Now for the rest of the Story". I now know what it was like to have strapped on a gun and pinned on a badge because I did become a LAWMAN. I loved the time I spent in Law Enforcement. I admire the men and women who came before me and the ones who have followed in my footsteps. Thank you for wearing the badge. The law enforcement officers, who put their lives on the line each and every day to protect our communities, cities, and towns, are dedicated. They leave their families each day knowing they may not come home, but they are dedicated to their career in Law Enforcement. Sometimes after hearing of some police tragedy I get tears of respect, admiration, and remorse.

A majority of the following stories were within the jurisdiction (County) of a Florida Sheriff. Let's discuss a brief history of the Florida Sheriff. The Office of Sheriff in the State of Florida is authorized and established by the Constitution of 1885 under which our state government now operates. This constitution provides that a Sheriff shall be elected in each county for a term of four years and that his powers, duties, and compensation shall be prescribed by law. The first election of Sheriff was held in 1888 and regular elections have taken place every four years since that time. The term of the Office of Sheriff commences on the first Tuesday after the first Monday in January after his election. The office of Sheriff is one of ancient origin. The majority of the functions of the office have come down to us from customs of the common law. The Sheriff, at common law, was the keeper of his county. He is the conservator of the peace and executive officer of the courts. He enforces the criminal laws by the apprehension and arrest of violators. He attends the courts and preserves order therein, and carries out the orders of the court. He serves process by which people are brought into court, so that rights and liabilities may be determined, and he enforces liabilities as established by the court.

Many law abiding citizens spend a life time in a county without ever coming into contact with the Sheriff and, therefore, little realize the importance of the proper performance of his duties to their everyday lives. Strong local government depends upon the firm and efficient execution of laws and the preservation of the public welfare in the locality. These functions are the chief responsibility of the Sheriff.

OATH OF OFFICE - Before entering upon the discharge of his official duties, the Sheriff is required to take and subscribe to the oath required by the Constitution, as follows: "I do solemnly swear (or affirm) that I will support, protect, and defend the Constitution and Government of the United States and the State of Florida; that I am duly qualified to hold office under the constitution of the state, and that I will and faithfully perform the duties of Sheriff of (*name of county*) County on which I am now about to enter. So help me God."

When the Sheriff takes the oath of office, the office becomes not so much a property right to be enjoyed by the Sheriff, as it is an obligation which he owes the State to discharge the duties and exercise the powers of Sheriff.

No society has survived unless it had reasoned peace. The police system today has an old English heritage.

Law enforcement as we know it now started in the seventh century in France. Thus we can see the legal beginning of the fine, restitution, involuntary servitude and rendition. The Frank-Pledge system was a method of establishing the responsibility of each man for his neighbor, and of a group for each man. It resulted in the development of the English borh and tithing system which was utilized to ensure local justice and to protect the community from raiding tribes.

Free men were required to group themselves into tithing, or group of ten families, for the purpose of maintaining the peace and sharing the duty of protecting the community. Each member of the tithing was responsible for the good behavior of his neighbor, and the tithing was responsible for the conduct of its members.

A "Headborough" or "Borsholder" or "Tithingman" was elected from the group and was given the responsibility for raising the hue and cry and meting out punishment. (The hue and cry was a process whereby every able bodied man had to join in the common chase for offenders.) Such activity was the origin of our current process of citizen's arrest.

Ten tithings were called a hundred. The head-man of a hundred was called a reeve. These hundreds eventually began to meet every month, and some commentators have called this the earliest beginning of the town meeting.

The constable (from the French institution comes stabuli, "master of the horse"; the Constables of France had the duty of raising and maintaining the armies) was given the duty of supervising the weapons and equipment of the hundred. Later, High Constables were appointed over hundreds and petty constables for towns and parishes within the hundred.

Several hundred formed a **shire**, a geographical area equivalent to a county. The headman of the **shire** was called a **shire-reeve** (from which the word "**Sheriff**" was derived), and became a powerful military and judicial official appointed by noblemen, or by the king in areas not owned by noblemen. **Shire-Reeves** held the power of posse comitatus (power of the county) by which they called upon all able-bodied men in the shire for assistance. Even today, in the United States, the County Sheriffs of most counties have a general power such as that. **THE SHERIFF.**

I hope after you read this book; you can see some of the humor and tragedy associated with Law Enforcement. You will read stories, some not so humorous, that tell of real life occurrences which happened to people due to their bad choices in life. As you know there are choices and there are consequences. You will also read that Law enforcement can be and is a dangerous career path. There is a gap between good and evil that law enforcement must fill. I have always believed it takes a special type of person to be a law enforcement officer.

"Make yourself familiar with the angels, and behold them frequently in spirit; for without being seen, they are present." I do believe in God and His guardian angels. During my career in law enforcement, I believe they were on my side many times, even before I was a Christian. Now I proudly say, I am a Christian.

There are four names of God in the Psalms that describe aspects of God's protection over us:

- ➢ "Most High" – shows Him to be greater than any threat we face.
- ➢ "Almighty" – emphasizes His power to confront and destroy every enemy
- ➢ "The Lord" – assures us that His presence is always with us
- ➢ "My God" – expresses the truth that God has chosen to associate intimately with those who trust Him.

"We have such a High Priest who is set on the right hand of the throne of the Majesty in the Heavens." Hebrews 8:1

"For he will command his angels concerning you, to guard you in all your ways; they will lift you up in their hands, so that you will not strike your foot against a stone." Psalm 91:11-12

To all past, present and future Law Enforcement Officers, I Truly respect you for the career you had, have, or are going to choose. I hold you up to God, and ask for your protection.

Prayer for Law Enforcement Officers

Dear Heavenly Father,

I thank you for the men and women that choose to run toward the dangerous situations in our world while others are running away. Thank you Lord for the people that dedicate their lives for the purpose of protecting others. I pray that you will protect them, give them wisdom and courage as they carry out their duties, and give them peace and rest when they are home. Protect their families from the trials that come from the life of an officer.

To the fallen officers Lord, I pray that their names will never be forgotten and that their life will always be honored.

Most of all, I pray for you to remove the divisions between our officers and our community. I pray for true unity and love for one another. Help us all to see each other as your children and not as enemies.

Show me Lord how I may best serve the ones that protect and serve me.

In Jesus name I pray, Amen.

By: Pastor Wesley S. Stanley (author's son)

"Remember ever; and always, that your country was founded…
by the stern old puritans who made the deck of the Mayflower
an altar of the Living God, and whose first act on touching the
soil of the new world was to offer on bended knees, thanksgiving
to Almighty God."

Henry Wilson, 18th U.S. Vice President under Ulysses S. Grant

CHARACTERS & LOCATIONS

Tomahawk County Sheriff's Department
City of Seminole as County Seat

Characters:

Sgt. Stoney Burke	Shift Supervisor
Summer Knight	Sheriff's Dispatcher
Tanya Young	Sheriff's Dispatcher
Sheriff Lance Rogers	Sheriff of Tomahawk County
Deputy Celina Adams	Patrol Deputy
Major Ron Edwards	Investigations Division Supervisor
Deputy James Roe	Patrol Deputy
Deputy Bobby Caruso	Patrol Deputy
Deputy John Earl	Patrol Deputy
Lt. Maurice Taylor	Patrol Shift Supervisor
Captain Bob Evans	Narcotic Division Supervisor
Deputy Ethan Davis	K-9 Officer (K-9 Apache)
Officer Tom Hill	Seminole Police Department Officer

Officer Brian Griffin	Seminole Police Department Officer
Dr. Jim Hook	Medical Examiner
Counselor Joe Rogers	Attorney/Judge

Cities:

Seminole
Cherokee
Muckville
Garnet
Renegade

Bars:

Gatorbait
Swamp Thing
Gatorland

Hospital:

Seminole Memorial Hospital in Seminole

INTRODUCTION

Sgt. Stoney Burke had been a Deputy Sheriff for fifteen years with the Tomahawk County Sheriff's Department, headquartered in the City of Seminole, which is the County seat of Tomahawk. This jurisdiction is located in the Deep South. The county is comprised of small towns and communities with rural surrounding areas, ranging from poverty stricken migrant camps to large sprawling farms and ranch estates. Stoney Burke was a Patrol Sergeant, Field Training Officer (FTO) and on the departments S.W.A.T. team. Earlier in his career he had worked as a K-9 officer, investigator, marine patrol officer, and a motorcycle officer, but he loved the patrol division. He felt at home working in patrol. Sgt. Burke loved working for Sheriff Lance Rogers, who had been the Sheriff in Tomahawk County for twenty-four years. Sgt. Burke's dad was a good friend of Sheriff Rogers. Sgt. Burke had grown up as friends with the Sheriff's son, Joe Rogers. During his early years growing up, Stoney thought he might want to become a police officer. He always wanted to know what it would be like to strap on a gun, pin on a badge, and become a lawman. Both Stoney and Joe had played football and baseball while attending high school. They were very close friends over the years. Upon graduation Joe attended college and later became a lawyer in his home town of Seminole. Stoney joined the U.S.

Army. After his enlistment was over, Stoney decided to act on his early dream to become a lawman. Stoney attended the police academy and then started working as a Deputy for the Tomahawk County Sheriff's Department. He planned to make law enforcement his career. Stoney worked for many years and had been promoted to Patrol Shift Supervisor after serving in several other divisions within the department

The Sheriff's Department was growing and times were changing fast. Sheriff Lance Rogers decided to hire his first female Deputy, Celina Adams. She had been a police officer at a local police department for two years. Sgt. Burke was called to the Sheriff's office to meet Sheriff Rogers. That is when Stoney Burke and Celina Adams first met. Sheriff Rogers also decided to change the patrol units to a two-person patrol unit on a trial basis. That's how Sgt. Burke and Deputy Adams became partners and lifelong friends. Their radio call number would be Tomahawk 10. These stories are based on actual events as the author recalls them. The names have been changed to protect the officers, individuals, accused and arrested, as well as the towns and law enforcement agencies.

CHAPTER 1

A Push in to Custody

It had been an extremely hot and slow evening in the small southern county, and Deputy Celina Adams was in her third week of training with Sgt. Burke. They stopped at a corner market to grab a coke and to chat a while. After they returned to their patrol car Sgt. Burke swung the vehicle around to face the intersection. He noticed a car stop at the red light, the light turned to green, but the vehicle just sat there. Finally, the driver got out. It was a young man not much more than 20 years old. He began to walk around to the rear of the car.

Sgt. Burke got out of his cruiser and told Celina he would be right back. This guy looked like he needed some help. As he approached the dark colored Chevy Camaro on foot, Burke radioed in the tag number and advised the dispatcher he would be assisting a broken down motorist at the intersection of Main Street and 3rd Avenue. The young man told Sgt. Burke he didn't know what was wrong, the car just died on him. He asked for assistance pushing the car across the street to the Exxon station. Burke hollered at Celina, who by that time was standing outside the patrol car watching Sgt. Burke, and she ran over to help out. The young driver got into his vehicle to steer and Burke and Celina pushed the car across to the opposite corner, to the Exxon station. The driver advised Sgt. Burke he would call his father to come and assist him, as his father was a mechanic. Burke and Celina walked back to their car and departed the area. They had gotten about two blocks away and just started to advise the dispatcher they were back in service for calls, when the dispatcher crackled across the radio "Tomahawk 10 are you still with that vehicle?" Sgt. Burke responded "no, we're about two blocks away". Dispatcher Summer Knight said "Well you better get back in a hurry. That car was stolen from Muckville, just this morning."

Sgt. Burke quickly turned around and headed back to the Exxon station. He pulled his patrol car behind the Camaro and noticed the young car thief going through the trunk. As Sgt. Burke and Celina approached the driver he just glanced over his shoulder quickly and stated "officer everything is ok, the car is broken down, my father is on the way to give me a ride and two officers already helped me a few minutes ago". Sgt. Burke grabbed the young man stating "we will be the only ride you will need this evening". He placed the handcuffs on his wrists and advised the thief he was under arrest for grand theft auto. He was also advised by Deputy Celina Adams of his Miranda rights. He was transported to the county jail and booked for grand theft auto. It was a Good evening. The deputies were at the right place at the right time. Case closed by arrest.

"He who has been stealing must steal no longer, but must work, doing something useful with his own hands, that he may have something to share with those in need." Ephesians 4:28

CHAPTER 2

Chance Happening-Purse Snatcher

Sgt. Burke and Deputy Adams were patrolling the north end of the county half way through the 3pm-11pm shift. They were traveling westbound on Renegade Road. It had been one of those quiet and boring night shifts so far. As they continued patrolling an unknown crime was occurring about a mile away. An elderly couple, Dick and Jane Parker were emerging from a store in the Universal Shopping Plaza at the corner of Park Road and Meridian Road. The Parkers were waiting for the walk light to cross Park Road northward to the west gate of the apartment complex where they lived.

Just before the Parkers were about to cross the road, Dick glanced over his shoulder and noticed a youth lurking in the darkened area a dozen feet behind them. As they attempted to cross, the youth ran and snatched Jane's pocketbook from her shoulder, knocking her to the ground. Dick turned and gave chase and fell in the soft sand. He picked himself up and gave chase again, shouting "Police-Help!". Dick chased the youth into the dark alley in back of the shopping plaza, where the youth got into the right passenger seat of a waiting red car. The red car took off with four young occupants. Dick was unable to obtain the license plate number. Breathless, Dick ran back to the store area to check on his wife and to call the Sheriff's Department. He reported the crime and gave a description of the purse snatch culprit, and said he had fled the scene in a red Ford with other occupants in the car. The dispatcher told Dick to stay where he was and that a patrol car would be there in a few minutes. She said they would also be sending an ambulance to check on his wife, who received a few scratches from her fall.

In their desperate rush to get away, the culprits in the red car were traveling at a high rate of speed southbound on Meridian Road. Sgt. Burke and Deputy Adams both observed this car run the red light at the corner of Renegade Road. Sgt. Burke stopped the red 4 door Ford, bearing a Florida tag, for the traffic violation.

Several young girls riding around the area at the time observed the purse snatcher running with Jane's pocketbook, and gave a short chase in their car. They were able to get the cars description and tag number. They returned to the scene of the purse snatching and met with Dick Parker. They gave Dick the information and he called the sheriff's department back and gave them the cars tag number. The three young female witnesses stayed until the deputy arrived.

As Deputy Adams was writing the driver of the red car a traffic citation for running the red light, the sheriff's dispatcher via police radio called a BOLO (be on the lookout) for a red Ford, and gave the reported tag number. She said the car was occupied by four young males in reference to a purse snatch/strong arm robbery which just occurred at the corner of Park Road and Meridian Road.

Sgt. Burke and Deputy Adams quickly realized their traffic stop was not merely a traffic violation but a crime. Sgt. Burke and Deputy Adams then arrested the cars four young occupants, recovered the stolen pocketbook, cash, and got a confession from the purse snatcher.

When Deputy James Roe arrived at the shopping plaza he told the Parkers of the apprehension of the four subjects and obtained a report from the Parkers as well as a statement from the three young females who had observed the crime.

Sgt. Burke and Deputy Adams transported the four youths to the shopping plaza where Dick Parker identified the one who snatched the pocketbook. The four young culprits were booked into the county jail.

In the words of Dick Parker "If I had seen such an episode on some TV police show program I would not have believed it to be a true happening, but it did in real life. The good Samaritans as witnesses, the quick work of the deputies, and police communications, and the speedy apprehension of the culprits all in a period of less than a half hour TV show, was and is to me almost incomprehensible in a real life crime".

Dick Parker also stated as a recent resident in the county, who had come from crime ridden New York, he wanted to thank all the deputies involved for their speedy and excellent effort. Mr. Parker also wrote a letter to Sheriff Rogers praising his Deputies and the work of the dispatcher on duty that night. Again, Deputies were at the right place at the right time. Case closed by Arrest.

"If you love me, keep my commandments" John 14:15

CHAPTER 3

Stolen Patrol Car

Law enforcement officers have always played practical jokes on fellow officers. Sgt. Burke surely did his share during his years. Most of the time it was to teach a valuable lesson to an officer. The Sheriff's Department had a deputy by the name of James Roe. Deputy Roe lived on the property of Seminole High School located in the county about a mile south of the town of Garnet. Deputy Roe took pride in doing extra patrols and checking out the school to prevent vandalism, burglaries and thefts from occurring. Sgt. Burke noticed that on the night shift, every time there was a silent alarm at the school, Deputy Roe would respond and park his patrol car under the same oak tree near the front of the school. He would get out of his car and run into the school leaving the car door partially open and the keys in the ignition. Sgt. Burke had gotten on to Deputy Roe several times in reference to this matter, but never wrote a formal reprimand or took it to a higher level by telling the Patrol Captain.

One night Sgt. Burke decided he would hopefully solve the problem about the key left in the ignition. He got with the Sheriff's Department night dispatcher. The Plan-- A fake school silent alarm would be dispatched to Deputy Roe at a certain time, only if it was not a busy night. The sheriff's dispatcher also contacted the dispatcher from the nearby town of Garnet who was a friend of Sgt. Burke. She agreed to be a partner in their little plan. Approximately 15 minutes prior to the time of the fake silent alarm call, Deputy Adams dropped off Sgt. Burke at Seminole High School near the oak tree. Sgt. Burke climbed up into the tree.

The fake call was dispatched. Several minutes later Deputy Roe and Deputy Bobby Caruso arrived at the school. As usual he parked under the oak tree and he and his partner ran into the school, towards the office, and out of sight. The car door, was as usual, open and keys left in the ignition. Sgt. Burke jumped down out of the tree, got into the patrol car and drove off. He drove the car and parked it in the rear parking lot of the Sheriff's Department. Deputy Adams picked him up.

Approximately 20 minutes later Deputy Roe called for unit Tomahawk 10 (Sgt. Burke) to respond to Seminole High School. When Sgt. Burke and Deputy Adams arrived, Deputy Roe slowly walked over to their car and said "my patrol car has been stolen". Sgt. Burke asked Roe if he was sure where he had parked his car. Roe stated "yes, I also left my keys in the ignition. Am I going to get fired"? Sgt. Burke said "I really don't know but probably so, due to your previous warnings".

Sgt. Burke and Deputy Adams then transported Deputy Roe and his partner, Deputy Caruso back to the Sheriff's Department. Burke told his dispatcher to call the surrounding police agencies and advise them that one of their patrol cars had been stolen. Approximately 25 minutes later, the dispatcher from the Garnet Police Department (their partner in this hoax) called the Sheriff's Department and advised them that one of their officers had found their stolen patrol car partly submerged in a canal in their city.

Sgt. Burke told Deputies Adams and Caruso to stay there and he was going to take Deputy Roe to Garnet to check on the patrol car. Deputy Roe was in tears by this time, knowing for sure now he would be fired. When they left the parking lot Sgt. Burke drove to the rear of the Sheriff's Department and pointed to Roe's patrol car---All safe. Sgt. Burke gave Deputy Roe his car keys and crawled his butt. No other reprimand was needed.

Deputy Roe never left his keys in his patrol car after that night and always locked his doors when he got out of the car. It was a hard way to learn a lesson but it worked. Deputy Roe thanked Sgt. Burke later, because he knew he could have been fired that night. Lesson learned.

"Give instruction to a wise man, and he will be still wiser; teach a righteous man, and he will increase in learning." Proverbs 9:9

CHAPTER 4

Officer Down- Code 3

Sgt. Burke was working the midnight shift on an extremely slow evening. It was approximately 2:25 a.m. and there were no other vehicles on the roadway. Sgt. Burke turned off his headlights, which is a common police tactic to covertly move around the area without being detected. He was patrolling very slowly north bound on Gator Tail Lane with the driver's window down. This was an area of numerous businesses and strip malls in the small community of Renegade.

As Sgt. Burke passed the Renegade Veterinary office, he believed he heard what appeared to be glass breaking from behind the building. Sgt. Burke drove past the office and stopped. The Sgt. called the information in to the dispatcher and parked his car. Burke then exited the patrol car and slowly walked back to the veterinary office. He started to walk around the building to check it out. As he rounded the back corner he spotted three males attempting to break into the rear door. They spotted Burke and took off running. The three suspects ran northwest and Sgt. Burke followed in foot pursuit. As he ran, Burke called via radio that he was chasing three subjects on foot toward the railroad tracks. He advised the dispatcher the three were all approximately sixteen to nineteen years of age, all wearing black or dark colored clothing. A minute later, Burke ran around the corner of a building and was hit in the face with a hard object. Burke staggered about eight to ten feet and immediately fell and landed face down on the railroad tracks. He was bleeding badly from a large gash in his face. The dispatcher attempted to call Sgt. Burke "Tomahawk 10" no answer, "Tomahawk 10" no answer. Deputy Celina Adams was already headed that way, approximately two miles away. Deputy Adams and several other deputies found Sgt. Burke about 15 minutes later. Burke was lying on the tracks, face down and was unconscious and bleeding badly from a head wound. Deputy Adams called by radio. "OFFICER DOWN, need back up and an ambulance CODE 3" and then gave the dispatcher and other responding deputies the exact location where Sgt. Burke was down, so they could spread out and look for the three suspects.

The next thing Sgt. Burke remembered was waking up in an air flight helicopter, on the way to the Seminole Memorial Hospital. The trip to the hospital was about 20 miles. The air flight EMT crew was working on Sgt. Burke, trying to stop the bleeding and keep him breathing.

Sgt. Burke was checked out at the hospital where lots of tests were run but fortunately no skull fracture. He had a large knot on his head, numerous stitches, and was black and blue with bruises. He was kept in the hospital for several days for observation. Sgt. Burke was not fond of the hospital stay, but he was grateful for the good care he received from his nurse, Madison.

Lt. Maurice Taylor, who had responded to the scene initially, proceeded to Sgt. Burke's residence to tell his wife, Sara about Stoney. At the residence, Burke's wife was advised of the situation, and then transported to the hospital by Lt. Taylor to see her husband.

Back at the scene that night Deputy Adams found a five-foot piece of lead pipe with wet blood on it near where Sgt. Burke fell on the tracks.

It was on this night in the helicopter when Sgt. Burke became a Christian. He had grown up attending church periodically. But on this night, he prayed and asked God to save him, confessed he was a sinner and asked the Heavenly Father to come into his life and forgive him of all his sins. Something good came out of a bad situation. Thank you Lord.

Deputy Roe and Caruso apprehended the three suspects hiding in a railroad car. Later, a finger print taken off the lead pipe was matched to one of the suspects. And the blood found on the pipe was matched to Sgt. Burke. That night investigators obtained confessions from all three suspects. Case closed by arrest.

OFFICER DOWN, two words that a law enforcement officer hates to hear come over the radio. They know that a fellow officer is hurt and needs help. It's time to pray. Most of the times responding officers feel so helpless because they are far away, and it seems like their patrol car cannot go fast enough to get to the fallen officer.

"The Lord is my strength and my shield, my heart trusts in him, and I am helped. My heart leaps for joy and I will give thanks to him in song." Psalm 28:7

CHAPTER 5

Rookie's first Night

Sgt. Burke was called into the Sheriff's office one morning and was told that he would be training a new recruit, who had recently graduated from the police academy. Sgt. Burke enjoyed the job of training new deputies. That's why he became a field training officer years before. He would be training Deputy John Earl starting tonight on the 3-11 shift.

Sgt. Burke had known Deputy Earl for approximately four years. When they first met, Earl was a manager at a fast food restaurant in the small town of Garnet. Earl later worked a short period for a security company before being accepted into the police academy.

Sgt. Burke liked Deputy Earl. He thought he was a quiet, shy young man that would probably make a good officer. On this extremely hot summer day Sgt. Burke and Earl met at roll call. After the short briefing, Sgt. Burke noticed that Deputy Earl was all spit and polished, clean cut hair, shoes shined and looking good. He was ready to set the world on fire with all his police learning and solve all the crime the county could throw at him. As Burke and Earl got in to the patrol car, to start their shift, Burke couldn't help to think back to his high school days. The time he thought about being a law enforcement officer someday. Sgt. Burke believed that Deputy Earl was thinking the same thing this very minute. Realizing his dream of what it would be like to strap on a gun, pin on a badge, and become a LAWMAN!

As they drove out of the Sheriff's Department parking lot, Sgt. Burke looked at Earl and said "forget everything you learned in the police academy, your real training starts today with me, on the job training". Burke then told Earl to be observant as they patrol the county and listen and watch him when they make contact with people. The next words that came out of Sgt. Burke were "this is real police work, not like a lot of the cop shows like Adam 12". You know the ones where an officer receives a call, answers the call and within a few minutes he solves the case and makes an arrest.

Sgt. Burke looked back in time, from all his years of experience. He had always had police street smarts and it seemed he was often in the right spot at the right time. And several times, the right spot at the wrong time!

As Sgt. Burke drove, Earl had lots of rookie questions. Burke also went over a lot of the department rules and regulations. They talked about procedures and how to handle traffic stops.

A short time later, after the rookie talk, the dispatcher gave out a BOLO (be on the lookout) for a signal 10 (stolen vehicle). The dispatcher then gave out the complete description of the car to include the year, make, model, color and tag number. About the time she finished broadcasting the BOLO information, Sgt. Burke looked up and the stolen car was driving by them as they sat at a red light. Sgt. Burke pulled behind the vehicle and verified the tag number with the dispatcher. He then told Deputy Earl, when they stop the vehicle to get out and stand behind the patrol car door on his side and cover him with his weapon. Sgt. Burke then turned on the overhead red and blue lights to stop the vehicle. The vehicle accelerated, turned a corner too fast and hit a telephone pole. The driver was ordered out of the car at gun point and handcuffed. As Sgt. Burke and Deputy Earl talked to the man, he got so scared he relieved himself. Burke looked down and the man was standing in his waste. The suspect was arrested and transported to the county jail and charged with grand theft auto.

Sgt. Burke and Deputy Earl then continued on patrol. During the next 6 hours, they were dispatched to several more calls; a bar fight, a business burglary and a domestic violence call. On all three calls, they responded, and arrests were made within minutes—Cases closed.

You can imagine how Deputy Earl felt, his first night as an officer. Boy this is great, how exciting! It does not get any better than this! Earl said "I am a lawman!" Burke remembered his High school dream. Sgt. Burke said to Earl "this was beginners luck". Sgt. Burke then told himself at the end of the shift, boy that rookie talk went to hell. Everything he had told Earl that would not happen, actually did happen. Deputy Earl turned out to be a good officer.

A few years later he went to work for a large Sheriff's Department in South Florida and eventually retired. Sgt. Burke and Earl have remained friends for over 40 years.

"Listen to advise and accept instruction, that you may gain wisdom in the future." Proverbs 19:20

Chapter 6

Phantom Shooter

Sgt. Burke was on patrol on the south edge of the city of Cherokee, a rural farming area. It was approximately 3:15 a.m. and extremely foggy as was often the case in this part of the county (south Florida, the everglades area).

As nature called, Sgt. Burke pulled his car off the side of the road and turned off the head lights. Stepping out of the car, he saw he was alone on the dark road and began to take care of his business.

He started to zip his pants up and something caught his eye in the distant shadows of the corn field. Looking more closely it appeared to be a silhouette of a light colored small car. In the stillness of the night he thought he faintly heard voices coming from the same area. As was procedure and Burke being safety conscious, he got on his police radio and asked his buddy Lieutenant Maurice Taylor, also working the grave yard shift to meet him at this location.

Lt. Taylor arrived about ten minutes later and joined Sgt. Burke outside his cruiser. Burke advised Taylor what he had seen and possibly heard. They both listened attentively, and suddenly a gunshot exploded breaking the stillness of the night. This sent both officers to the prone position, fighting for a spot as they belly crawled to a safe place behind the patrol car tires.

After that first instant of survival instinct overwhelmed them, they remembered they were officers and attempted to regain some dignity by crawling out on the back side of the car and taking cover. Sgt. Burke drew his service weapon, a Beretta 40 Caliber semi-auto pistol, from his holster and shouted "police, come out where we can see you with your hands up"! Another shot rang threw the air and a muzzle flash was seen by the officers. Burke and Taylor both returned fire. A third shot rang out. They looked at each other in disbelief. They couldn't just stand there and keep shooting at someone they couldn't even see.

Ok Burke said, time for a coin toss. He flipped the quarter into the air and as he caught it and turned it over on his hand he realized he had lost. He would be the one to move in closer, under cover of dark and fog, to try to get an eye on what in the world they had come against. Lt. Taylor of course would be keeping a watchful eye and covering him from the safety and protection of the parked patrol cars.

Sgt. Burke took a deep breath and got as close as he could to the ground before silently creeping to the edge of the field. Still being unable to make out what was in the distance; he again resorted to the belly crawl and inched his way in closer. When he was within what he felt to be about twenty yards of the area, he cautiously raised his head to peer between the corn stalks. A forth shot blasted, and just before he unloaded his pistol at the area of the vehicle and muzzle flashes, his eyes became accustomed to what he was seeing. Burke shouted to Lt. Taylor, "it's safe and get out here!"

Much to their embarrassment, the phantom shooter turned out to be a propane powered mechanism, designed to blast at different intervals, to scare off birds and any other critters that may be hazardous to the crop. This contraption was mounted to the back of a light colored pickup truck.

They chuckled to themselves, and were silently appreciative that this would only be between the two of them.

It was only a couple of hours later; over their morning cup of coffee that it occurred to them that they were their biggest danger. They had been shooting toward a propane gas tank! This was not a story they would be taking home to their wives. If they had hit the propane tank with a bullet, it would have exploded. They did what they thought was right at the time, but what fools they turned out to be. As you know there are always those Monday morning quarterbacks. However, they were safe and able to go home another day.

Lt. Taylor and Burke knew they could not keep this to themselves. They had fired their weapons. The Captain, Major and the Sheriff were notified of the incident. They wrote their necessary report. They got lots of laughs and kidding from their fellow Deputies. The local newspaper also got their shot at them. The headlines read, "Miniature war flares in corn field". They also had their laughs. In the end, they were safe.

"The horse is prepared against the day of battle; but safety is of the Lord." Proverbs 21:31

CHAPTER 7

Bombed from Above

Sgt. Burke taught another hard learned lesson. Practical jokes continued on Deputy James Roe. He did not always make safety a top priority when answering alarm calls. This made Sgt. Burke furious, fearing for the safety of him and others. Deputy Roe would exit his patrol car with a cup of coffee in one hand and a cigarette in the other, having no free hands. This could be very dangerous.

Again and again Sgt. Burke counseled Deputy Roe on the bad habits that he had picked up. That it could be fatal one day. Sgt. Burke wanted his officers to always be safety conscious. Deputy Roe was an older officer, and was a little lazy, but Sgt. Burke liked him a lot and believed he could shape him into a good officer. However, Deputy Roe continued the bad habit of having no free hands on alarm calls.

Sgt. Burke, Deputy Celina Adams and two other Deputies decided to play another practical joke on poor Deputy Roe.

This would be a good night, as Roe's partner had called in sick and Roe would be alone.

It was an extremely cold winter night in January, working the hated midnight shift. Sgt. Burke told his deputies during roll call that the 3-11 shift had been very quiet. He told his shift to get out there and check their assigned zones really good for about two hours. If it remained quiet, he would start one by one conducting his monthly patrol car inspections. This was also a hint for them to clean up their patrol cars if needed. Inspections were usually unannounced but Sgt. Burke was in a good mood.

Sgt. Burke then walked into the dispatch room while his officers started their shift. Burke told his dispatcher if it was quiet at 3:00 a.m. to dispatch Deputy Roe to the Gatorbait Bar, which closes at 2:00 a.m. The Gatorbait bar is located at the end of a strip mall on Seminole Highway just outside the town of Garnet.

It was a very slow and quiet shift. At 2:45 a.m. Sgt. Burke, Deputies Adams, Black and Caruso met one block from the Bar. They walked to the bar, each carrying four water balloons. They climbed to the top of the bar, lying in wait for Roe. At 3:00 Deputy Roe was dispatched to a fake silent alarm call at the Gatorbait Bar. Sgt. Burke advised the dispatcher, by radio, that he would be heading toward the bar as back up, to make the call sound realistic.

As Deputy Roe arrived, he parked right in front of the bar. He exited the car and as expected, Sgt. Burke saw Roe with a cigarette in one hand and a cup of coffee in the other.

Deputy Adams threw the first balloon striking Roe center mass in the chest area. The rest of the deputies let loose with their water balloons, with Roe as the target. Most of the balloons hit their intended target. Deputy Roe dropped his coffee and cigarette and dove back into his patrol car and drove off, not saying a word to the dispatcher. After several minutes he called the dispatcher saying everything was ok and he would be back in service. Sgt. Burke advised the dispatcher he would also be back in service since all was ok at the bar.

Sgt. Burke and the other Deputies continued their patrol duties. About 40 minutes later Deputy Roe called Sgt. Burke on the radio and asked him to meet him for breakfast at the all night restaurant. He needed to give him some important information. When they arrived at the restaurant Sgt. Burke, and Deputy Adams met Deputy Roe inside for breakfast. Deputy Roe was completely dried off; he had changed his uniform. Roe told Sgt. Burke, "I know that was you". Sgt. Burke said "what are you talking about"? Roe continued to say "ok you taught me another hard lesson, which might save my life someday". Deputy Roe gave up cigarettes. He still drinks coffee. However, Sgt. Burke never saw Roe get out of his patrol car on a call with coffee in his hand. Another lesson learned, the hard way, but learned.

"Now these things happen to them as an example, but they were written down for our instruction, on whom the end of the ages has come." 1 Corinthians 10:11

CHAPTER 8

Day Shift Trouble

Day shift, yuk, well somebody had to do it. It was time for Sgt. Burkes squad to rotate to day shift. Sgt. Burke did not like the day shift; he hated the traffic, and all the department brass was in the office, listening to everything that comes across the radio. Not that this was a big deal since nothing ever happened around here in the middle of a bright summer day.

Deputy Celina Adams thought she would just go patrol the school zone, and then head out to Highway 103 to write a few speeding citations, to unsuspecting motorists, to pass the time away. Just think, in three more months she would be back on the evening shift she loved, where the real police work took place.

"Celina", Sgt. Burke shouted as she walked past his office door to leave the building. "It's very wet out their due to the recent rain, stay out of the median on Highway 103, you'll get bogged down. You can drive down to the next cross over to switch lanes. Don't make me have to come out there and get you hauled out of the median by a wrecker." Deputy Adams spoke over her shoulder as she walked out of the office, "sure Sergeant, no problem".

Two hours later she had herself set up just over the hill where her patrol car couldn't be spotted until you topped the hill, and then it was too late. Her radar would have already registered the speed and you know the rest of the story. Can you say citation?

She hadn't been sitting there five minutes when a black Chevrolet corvette topped the hill. The radar let out a high pitched squeal and triple digits registered on the radar readout panel. She could not believe her luck or what she saw; 103 MPH (miles per hour).

Fortunately, the corvettes driver, seeing the patrol car pulling onto the roadway, pulled off on the side of the road. Otherwise he probably would have never been caught.

The citation was written and issued for unlawful speed and Deputy Adams wished Mr. Peterson a good day. As she pulled her patrol car back onto the roadway; she considered the mile she would have to drive to reach the paved turn around. She didn't have time for that. She was a busy woman with speeders to chase. She would just jump across the median right here. It looked hard and harmless to her.

She shot across the road and into the grassy median. The patrol car rolled down one side and headed up the other, and then the rear tires started to spin. "Holy cow" she said to herself as the sergeant's words echoed in her head. "Don't panic, just keep it moving" she thought. As the back tires continued to spin the forward progression became slower and slower, until finally she felt the sinking of the rear end of the car just prior to it coming to a complete halt. She put it in reverse and then back into drive, but all in vain. The car was stuck; all she was doing now was spinning. Oh my gosh. What was he, (Burke) going to have to say about this.

Deputy Adams just sat in the patrol car for about thirty minutes before she got the nerve to call for help on the radio. She had prayed that a wrecker would have driven by and she could flag him down. That way, no one would have to know, would they?

She finally gave it up, swallowed crow and asked Sgt. Burke via police radio to meet her up on Highway 103 two miles north of Seminole. When he arrived 45 minutes later, he had a wrecker with him. How did you know? Burke just shook his head, got into his car and drove off.

Nothing was ever said, but when asked if Celina Adams learned her lesson, the answer would have to be yes. Sgt. Burke always seemed to be right and have all the answers. During his earlier years, Sgt. Burke had been there and done that. He walked the walk and talked the talk. He made his share of mistakes, however he learned from his mistakes. She knew he was a great supervisor, and she admired him as a man and a law enforcement officer.

"I will instruct you and teach you in the way you should go; I will counsel and watch over you." Psalm 32:8

CHAPTER 9

Gunman Walking Down Road

While on the day shift, Sgt. Burke was sitting at his desk at the Sheriff's Department catching up on reports, checking reports, and other misc. paper work, before heading back out to patrol the county. At 11:48 a.m. Sgt. Burke received a phone call from Summer, his favorite dispatcher from the Sheriff's Department. She advised Burke she had received a man with a gun complaint from a motorist out on Canal Street, which was in Zone 2 of the divided county area. Burke knew the Deputy working that zone had earlier arrested a man for grand theft and was busy at the county jail booking the prisoner. Burke advised the dispatcher he would handle the call, but also have Deputy John Earl, in Zone 3 head that way for backup in case he needed help. He further advised the dispatcher to wait until he got in his patrol car to give out the information and description of the man. Sgt. Burke immediately left the Sheriff's Office and advised the dispatcher he was in his car and in service. The dispatcher via police radio then gave out a BOLO (be on lookout) for a Mexican Male, approximately 5'9", 160 pounds, short black hair, last seen wearing blue jeans, white tennis shoes, and a dark blue football jersey with the number eighty-one in white on the front and rear. He was armed with a dark colored revolver in his right hand. The subject was walking south bound along Canal Street waving the gun around in the air and at people as they drove past him. He was last seen approximately two and a half miles south of the city limits of Seminole.

Sgt. Burke advised the dispatcher he would be in route to the Canal Street area. He also knew that there were numerous residences in the area as well as a few stores and a bank.

Sgt. Burke arrived in the area about 6 minutes later and did not observe the subject. He continued to drive south bound on Canal Street for approximately five miles and still did not observe the subject. Burke turned around and headed back toward town. He figured he would check the bank, stores and around the residential area for the subject.

As Sgt. Burke got near the bank he observed the subject matching the description the dispatcher had given him. The male was now walking north bound along the west side of the south bound lane of Canal Street. He was not carrying his revolver in his hand. He was now holding what appeared to be a can of soda in his left hand. Sgt. Burke eased up behind the subject and noticed the hand grip of the revolver sticking out of the subject's right front pants pocket. Burke stopped his patrol car approximately fifteen yards behind the subject who was still walking. Burke exited his car, pulled his Beretta 40 caliber pistol out of his holster and pointed it at the subject who had not yet seen him. Burke yelled "FREEZE". The male subject looked back at

Burke, then reached down and grabbed the revolver with his right hand and pulled it out, but he was still facing away from Burke. Burke ordered him to drop the gun, or be shot. Burke did not know if the man even spoke English. The subject continued to turn the gun toward Burke. Just as Sgt. Burke started to squeeze his trigger and shoot the man in the upper chest, the armed man dropped his gun and Burke did not shoot. A split second, good decision. The gun dropped to the pavement of the road and bounced. Sgt. Burke heard the noise of the gun hitting the road and knew it was a toy gun, a plastic toy gun.

Sgt. Burke ran over and grabbed the man, who began to struggle as Burke attempted to handcuff him. The man started to swing his fist and kick Burke to avoid arrest. Burke forced the man off his feet and onto the ground where he continued to resist being handcuffed. Burke finally got him handcuffed behind his back as Deputy John Earl arrived on the scene. Deputy Earl helped the man up to his feet, and then placed him in the rear seat of Burke's patrol car. He then walked over to check on Sgt. Burke who was still on his knees on the ground. Burke said "getting old". He was starting to feel sick, apparently from getting too hot during the struggle and the adrenaline that was flowing through his body at the time.

Sgt. Burke knew that he almost killed a man over a plastic toy gun that looked very real, especially when it started to be pointed at him. Burke said to himself "another second and he would have shot the man". Burke also knew if he had shot the man, he would have been cleared by the State

Attorneys investigation. Burke knew he was in fear of his life, at the time. Burke told Deputy Earl "it was going to be him or me, and I was going to go home". Burke continued to tell Deputy Earl "I'd rather be judged by twelve, than carried by six".

Deputy Earl continued on patrol and Sgt. Burke transported the subject to the county jail, where he was charged with improper exhibition of a firearm and resisting arrest with violence. Case closed by arrest.

Sgt. Burke finished the booking of the prisoner into the county jail, just in time to make it to the supervisor's meeting with Sheriff Rogers at 2:00 p.m.

"As I live, saith the Lord God. I have no pleasure in the death of the wicked, but that the wicked turn from his way and live; turn ye, turn ye, from your evil way; for why will ye die-oh house of Israel." Ezekiel 33:11

CHAPTER 10

Cherry Picker Drug Raid

While walking down the hall at the Sheriff's Office, Sgt. Burke ran into Sheriff Rogers. The Sheriff told Burke to call Captain Bob Evans, the narcotic unit supervisor for the department. When Burke called Captain Evans, on that Thursday morning, the Captain asked him to meet with him at 1:00 p.m., downstairs in the narcotic division office. The Captain stated he needed some help and Sheriff Rogers had recommended him for the job.

When Burke met with Captain Evans, he was advised the narcotic unit had been working a drug case off and on for a year. Undercover agents had made numerous controlled buys of powder and crack cocaine from a female named Louise. Louise lived upstairs in apartment # 20 at the Shady Oaks Apartments. Shady Oaks was located at 1234 S.E. 4th Avenue in the community known as Broken Arrow. It was a run down, low income, trashy apartment complex. The apartment building was about ten feet off the roadway near two bars. Captain Evans stated they had obtained Search Warrants for the apartment several times, however, each time they would conduct the raid with the search warrant, Louise would jump up and run to her bathroom and flush her drugs down the toilet. The officers could only arrest her for the sale of cocaine to the undercover agents and CI's (confidential Informants) on the previous buy dates. After the long meeting with Captain Evans and his agents, they had a plan.

Captain Evans had obtained another arrest and search warrant that they would serve and execute on Louise and her apartment on Saturday evening at approximately 9:00 p.m.

Saturday evening was usually a big day for Louise; she was usually very busy selling her drugs out of her apartment. Captain Evans believed she probably got her drug supply on Friday night or Saturday from her drug supplier. At the present time the narcotic unit did not have a clue from whom or where she was getting her drugs. The narcotic agents had conducted surveillance on her and the apartment several times. They always observed lots of traffic going and coming in and out of her apartment. They could not tell who had brought her the cocaine.

Saturday evening finally arrived. Sgt. Burke was extremely excited to be working with the narcotic unit again. Burke met the agents at the narcotics unit at 7:00 p.m. He was dressed in blue jeans and a city utility shirt, as were the other officers. They were going to make out like they were the city crew, making repairs on some power lines using the cherry picker near the apartment complex. The cherry picker and their city crew clothing disguise should hopefully help them blend in enough to get through the drug raid without any suspicion. This plan of using a man in the cherry picker basket was to prevent Louise from flushing the cocaine down her bathroom toilet.

The cherry picker would get parked on S.E. 4th Avenue in front of the Shady Oaks Apartments, close to Louise's bathroom window. An agent in the cherry picker basket would raise himself up and over to just outside the window, near some power lines at the second floor level.

Sgt. Burke would be on the apartment entry team with four narcotic agents that would be wearing black masks to hide their identity. They would enter and secure the apartment, making sure all people in the apartment were secure and there were no weapons, and to make the place safe. Then search and secure all evidence. The man in the cherry picker basket would use a long wooden pole to bust through the bathroom window and push snugly against the bathroom door to secure it from the inside. This would prevent Louise from entering her bathroom and flushing the drugs down the toilet, as she has done on previous drug raids.

Nine p.m., raid time. The agents in the cherry picker drove around the corner and parked in place on S.E. 4th Avenue. They exited the truck and one agent got into the cherry picker basket and moved it into place near the bathroom window. The entry team had driven another city crew pickup truck and parked at one end of the apartment building. They exited the truck and quickly made their way upstairs to the area of apartment number twenty. At 9:10 the signal was given by Captain Evans, via police radio, to start the raid. Sgt. Burke utilized a large sledge hammer and yelled POLICE, SEARCH WARRANT, as he struck the door handle of apartment. This knocked the handle out of the door, and the door flew open. Sgt. Burke was the first officer to enter the apartment. He had dropped the sledge hammer and pulled his service weapon, his old trusty Beretta 40 Caliber pistol, out of its holster. As burke entered, he was immediately attacked by a large dog (Doberman Pincher). The dog started biting Burke all over his left arm and leg, where ever there was an opening. The other agents rushed in to secure the apartment and to get to Louise before she got to the bathroom. Louise jumped up from her chair, grabbed her cocaine and was running to the back of the apartment towards the bathroom. Sgt. Burke, who was getting eaten alive by the dog, had no alternative but to shoot him. One agent via police radio said "she's running towards the bathroom"! The bathroom door flew open and as Louise stepped into the room, Agent Hernandez took his long wooden poll, thrust it through the bathroom window, and ended up striking Louise between her eyes with the pole. She had already entered the bathroom and as the pole struck her, powder and crack cocaine went flying throughout the room. Hernandez was able to keep Louise away from the toilet until other officers reached her and took her into another room where she was handcuffed.

The only drugs found were the cocaine scattered all over the bathroom floor. Approximately one pound of cocaine was found and taken into evidence. Louise was arrested for the sale of cocaine, possession of cocaine with intent to sell, and possession of a firearm by a convicted felon. A gun was found under her pillow on her bed and another was found on the coffee table in the living room.

Sgt. Burke drove himself to the local hospital where he obtained a tetanus shot and received numerous stitches to close the wounds on his arm and leg. He recovered to fight another day. Another drug dealer was taken off the road. Case closed by arrest.

"In him we were also chosen, having been predestined according to the plan of him who works out everything in conformity with the purpose of his will." Ephesians 1:11

CHAPTER 11

Seventeen Bales of Marijuana

Prior to becoming a Sergeant, Stoney Burke was a Corporal and was the Department's K-9 Officer. He had a dog named Apache; a three-year-old male German shepherd. K-9 Apache was a patrol and narcotic detection dog.

Burke was also a certified K-9 instructor for both patrol and narcotic detection dogs. Burke worked hard with his K-9, three to four times a week, to keep Apache in top shape for patrol type cases (attack work, tracking, building searches, etc.). Burke was a member of the USPCA (United States Police Canine Association). Apache had also been certified by the USPCA in both patrol and narcotic detection. Burke and Apache had received numerous National Awards from the USPCA for making narcotics cases. Burke was very proud of his time in the K-9 Division; he loved dogs and especially working with Apache.

When Burke was advised he was going to be promoted to Patrol Shift Sergeant, he knew his K-9 days were going to be over. The Sheriff's Department put out a memo saying there would be an opening for a K-9 Officer, and anyone interested needed to contact Cpl. Burke. After a two-week period, Deputy Ethan Davis volunteered for the K-9 Officer position.

Deputy Davis was a young 24-year-old man; he had been a deputy for three years. He had joined the Sheriff's Department immediately after serving his country as a U.S. Marine and attending the police academy. Burke liked Davis, thought he was a good young officer and would be a good candidate for the K-9 position. Burke passed the transfer request up the chain of command. A week later, Sheriff Rogers called Cpl. Burke and Deputy Davis for a meeting. The Sheriff agreed to the transfer of Deputy Davis to the K-9 division, and also promoted Burke to Sergeant. Sheriff Rogers stated Burke would be supervising a patrol shift as soon as he got Deputy Davis trained to handle K-9 Apache. For the next month Sgt. Burke worked with Deputy Davis and K-9 Apache. They worked on attack work, building searches, tracking and narcotic detection for cocaine and marijuana. Finally, the day came when Sgt. Burke felt Deputy Davis and K-9 Apache were ready as a team and Sheriff Rogers gave the go ahead after watching the team demonstrate proficiency in all areas of K-9 handling. Sgt. Burke would take over the 3-11 shift from Sgt. Tom Weaver who had just retired. Deputy Davis and K-9 Apache would also be working the evening shift under Sgt. Burke.

Three weeks later, Officer Tom Hill from the Seminole Police Dept. was working a traffic accident at the intersection of highway 401 and Canal Street. A Ford Bronco pulling a closed in trailer occupied by a male driver and male passenger ran a red light and struck a Chevy 4 door sedan driven by an older female. Sgt. Burke just happened to drive by the accident about 10 minutes later. Officer Hill told Burke that the two men from the Bronco were acting very suspicious. The two men had both exited the Bronco. Sgt. Burke exited his patrol car and walked over to the Bronco to look. The passenger door just happened to be open. Burke observed from the outside of the vehicle several marijuana joints in the ashtray. Burke told Officer Hill, who then arrested the two men for possession of marijuana. He placed them in the back seat of his patrol car and continued to work the accident.

Sgt. Burke via police radio asked Deputy Davis and K-9 Apache to respond to the scene of the accident. Approximately 15 minutes later the K-9 team arrived at the scene. Sgt. Burke told Deputy Davis what had occurred and asked as a request from Officer Hill to have K-9 Apache sniff around the closed trailer. Deputy Davis got K-9 Apache out of the patrol car, put him on a leash and walked him to the area of the closed trailer. Davis gave Apache the command "find the dope". Apache walked around the trailer then stopped at the rear double door and stuck his nose in the crack of the door. Apache started scratching and biting at the rear door area. That was Apache's alert that he smelled drugs he was trained to detect. At that time Deputy Davis read the two men from the Bronco their Miranda Rights. He advised them that Apache was a certified narcotic detection dog, he had alerted to the trailer, and we were going to search the trailer for narcotics. Officer Tom Hill and Deputy Ethan

Davis opened the rear doors of the trailer while Sgt. Burke looked on. When the doors were opened the officers found a trailer full of large bales wrapped in burlap. Officer Hill took a photograph of the bales as they found them, then cut in to one of the bales and observed a green leafy substance they believed to be marijuana. A presumptive test was run on the substance by Deputy Davis. The test came back positive for marijuana. Officer Hill and Deputy Davis then entered the trailer and counted the bales. Seventeen bales!

The Ford Bronco and trailer were towed to the impound lot at the Seminole Police Department. Later the bales were weighed. Each was approximately 87 pounds with a total weight of 1,485 pounds. The two men from the Bronco were arrested for possession of marijuana with intent to sell and booked into the county jail.

Sgt. Burke was very proud of Deputy Davis and Apache. That was the team's first drug bust. Sgt. Burke called the Sheriff and advised him of the assistance given to the Seminole Police Dept. and about the drug bust.

Sgt. Burke wrote a letter of appreciation to Deputy Davis and Apache for a job well done. Case closed by arrest.

"In the same way, let your light shine before others, so that they may see your good works and give glory to your father who is in heaven." Matthew 5:16

Chapter 12

Hotel Fire Kills One, Injures Two

The early day shift hours started out extremely slow on this hot summer morning. Sgt. Burke patrolled the county stopping by several businesses to chat with the owners. He did this to help with the community policing that Sheriff Lance Rogers encouraged all his deputies to engage in. He wanted his deputies to get to know the people in their zones, and wanted the public to trust in his officers. He wanted his deputies to know what was happening in their assigned jurisdictions. Besides, Burke enjoyed this part of his job.

At approximately 11:25 a.m., Summer, the Sheriff Department's dispatcher, via police radio, broadcast a fire call at the Palms Hotel. The Palms Hotel was located in the community of Muckville. The hotel was a small old wooden two story building. The hotel only had 12 rooms. The 6 upstairs rooms were efficiency apartments and all rented out at the time of the fire.

Sgt. Burke and Deputy John Earl arrived at the same time as the first fire truck at approximately 11:38 a.m. The first floor was engulfed with fire and smoke was billowing out all of the windows. Burke told Deputy Earl to stop the traffic to allow other emergency vehicles in to the area. Burke walked around to the front side of the hotel and heard a male voice saying "help, help, help"! Burke looked up and observed an elderly man, later found to be Jeff Phillips. Phillips' upper body was stretching out the second floor bedroom window of his apartment and lots of smoke was coming out the window as well. Sgt. Burke looked around and then yelled to Deputy Earl for help. The two officers grabbed a ladder off the fire truck. They placed the ladder up against the front of the hotel near Phillips bedroom window. Deputy Earl held the ladder and Burke climbed up the ladder to Phillips who at that time was starting to suffer from smoke inhalation. Burke grabbed Phillips, pulled him out of the window, and placed him over his shoulders and carried him down the ladder to an awaiting ambulance EMT crew, which had observed the action upon their arrival at the scene.

Yelling and screaming was heard again from the 2nd floor. It appeared to be coming from the apartment to the left of Phillips apartment. Deputies Earl and Burke then moved the ladder over. Burke again climbed up the ladder to the bedroom window. Lots of smoke was coming out. Burke could hear a faint voice from inside the apartment. Sgt. Burked leaned through the window and grabbed another elderly man named Twigger Jones. Burke placed the man over his shoulder and carried him down the ladder. The EMTs were again waiting to render first aid to the second subject.

The fire was finally extinguished by the fire department. A later look and investigation at the scene of the fire revealed one deceased male in an upstairs back side apartment. All other occupants had gotten out without any injuries. Mr. Phillips and Mr. Jones were taken to the hospital and treated for smoke inhalation and released.

Later on Sgt. Burke received an award for saving the life of the two men at the hotel. Burke was appreciative of his award; however, he was extremely sad for the victim of the fire wishing he could have saved that man's life as well.

"He hears me when I weep. The Lord has heard my weeping. The Lord has heard my cry." Psalm 6:8-9

CHAPTER 13

Car Keys Get Officers Hurt

Late one Saturday afternoon in the early springtime, Summer, the department's dispatcher, sent out a call to Deputy John Earl. The call came across as "see a woman about her car keys at the Gator Tail Bar" which was located just north of the small town of Seminole. Deputy Earl advised the dispatcher he would be 10-51 (in route to the call). Sgt. Burke who was only about a mile away stated he was close to the bar, and would handle the call. Deputy Earl decided to continue heading that way.

When Burke arrived at the bar, a black female flagged him down in the parking lot. The female was known by Burke. Her name was Frances Green. Green was yelling, cursing, very upset, and appeared to be intoxicated. She told Burke that her ex-boyfriend, Otis Barlow, had stolen the keys of her 1978 Cadillac and he would not give them back to her. She continued to tell Burke that Otis had entered the bar and refused to talk to her or give the keys back. And he had pushed her out of the bar.

Burke knew of Otis Barlow. He had arrested him on numerous occasions, mostly for criminal mischief and intoxication type calls. As Burke spoke to Green, Deputy Earl arrived on the scene.

Sgt. Burke and Deputy Earl then decided to enter the bar in an attempt to speak to Otis Barlow. As the officers entered the bar, they observed Barlow playing a game of pool. He appeared to be intoxicated, as he was talking to others in the bar. He staggered as he walked around the pool table, and his speech was slurred. Burke knew there was going to be trouble from previous encounters with Barlow.

Sgt. Burke walked up to Barlow and asked him to step outside so they could talk. It was extremely noisy inside the bar. Barlow looked at Burke and stated "kiss my butt". Burke again requested that Barlow step outside. Barlow began to yell at both officers and then threw a beer bottle at Burke. At this time Burke and Earl both grabbed Barlow and advised him he was under arrest. As Burke attempted to handcuff Barlow, the lights went out in the bar, at which time another bar patron threw a beer bottle at Deputy Earl. The bottle hit, and exploded, on the grip of his service revolver which was strapped on his waist. The force of the thrown bottle sent splinters of broken glass into Deputy Earl's side. Sgt. Burke then felt several cuts on both his arms. When the lights came back on, Deputy Earl still had ahold of Barlow, and Frances Green was standing in front of Burke with a broken beer bottle in her right hand. As she stepped forward and attempted to cut Burke again he started backing up until his back was against the wall, and he could back no further. Burke noticed numerous people standing behind Green and he elected not to pull his service weapon and shoot, even though she was still attempting to cut him. Burke had his long c-cell flashlight in his hand. He drew back, swung, and struck Green between her eyes. She immediately fell to the floor. Sgt. Burke handcuffed Green and then turned his attention to Deputy Earl who was rolling around on the floor with Barlow. Sgt. Burke jumped in the mix, and he and Earl continued struggling with Barlow. They finally got him handcuffed, after several minutes of Barlow twisting, turning, kicking and hitting Burke and Earl in an attempt to get away and resist arrest.

Green was arrested for Aggravated Battery on a Law Enforcement Officer. Barlow was arrested for Intoxication and Resisting Arrest with Violence. Deputy Bobby Caruso who arrived at the bar transported both Barlow and Green to the County Jail. Both Sgt. Burke and Deputy Earl were treated outside the bar by EMT personnel. They drove themselves to the hospital where they received sutures to close wounds suffered during this simple call that turned violent. Case closed by arrest.

"Come, let us return to the Lord, he has torn us to pieces but he will heal us; he has injured us but will bind up our wounds." Hosea 6:1

CHAPTER 14

Tragic Accident Kills One

On this beautiful late afternoon, in September, Jane Jones and her mother were getting ready to go shopping at Wal-Mart, and then go out to eat together.

They left Elizabeth's house with Jane driving a white colored Toyota Camry. Elizabeth was sitting in the front passenger seat. Jane told her mother that they needed to stop and get gas. After leaving the house, they turned westbound on SR100 in the town of Renegade, heading for Seminole.

As they proceeded westbound on SR100, the sun was low in the sky and glaring in to Jane's eyes. It was hard for her to see, as they were about to top a small hill. Jane decided to turn left into the Tom Thumb Store for gas. As she turned, not seeing well, she turned the Toyota into the path of an 18-wheel semi-tractor truck, driven by Sean Evans. Sean was a young man from the town of Cherokee. The truck was traveling eastbound on SR100.

Sean Evans stomped on his brakes, causing his tires to lock up, leaving several yards of skid marks and gouges in the road. He was not able to stop his truck in time to prevent an accident.

The truck's right front bumper struck the Jones' Toyota in the area of the front passenger door. This probably killed Elizabeth instantly. The impact pushed the Toyota in a south east direction, in to numerous large trees. Sgt. Burke was only about half a mile away from the accident scene when the Sheriff's Department Dispatcher, Summer, via police radio, sent out the call of a Signal 4 (traffic accident) on SR100 and Pine Street, in front of the Tom Thumb Store. Sgt. Burke arrived on the scene about the time Summer finished broadcasting the accident. Sgt. Burke immediately asked for backup to control traffic, and the fire department to include EMTs and ambulances.

Burke first made contact with Sean Evans, the truck driver. He was shaken up but told Burke he wasn't injured. Burke then approached the Toyota and helped Jane who was exiting the car. Jane had numerous lacerations on her arms, head, and legs. Burke helped her to sit on the ground. EMT personnel had arrived and started working on Jane. Burke then walked over to check on Elizabeth who was still in the front passenger seat. She had a small amount of blood coming out of her right ear and right eye socket. She appeared to be deceased. Burke then asked for the EMT to check on Elizabeth. EMT Wesley Ward told Burke that Elizabeth was in fact deceased. Burke then advised Jane that her mother had been killed in the accident. Jane was transported to Seminole Memorial Hospital in the town of Seminole.

Other deputies had arrived on the scene. Burke told them to detour traffic from around the area, because they were going to be there awhile. Burke, who was also a traffic homicide investigator, began his investigation of the accident.

After several hours, the body of Elizabeth had to be cut out of the Toyota and she was transported to the morgue at Seminole Memorial Hospital in Seminole. The vehicles were then both towed from the scene to a local tow truck business impound lot.

After Burke's investigation, he concluded that the cause of the accident was the improper left turn, by Jane, into the Tom Thumb, with the sun being a contributing factor. Both Jane and Elizabeth were also not wearing seatbelts. According to witnesses and measurements, at the scene, Burke knew Sean Evans was driving the speed limit and could not prevent the impact with the Jones vehicle.

Sgt. Burke left the accident scene approximately four hours after the accident had occurred. He proceeded to Seminole Memorial Hospital to finish the investigation. Burke knew this was going to be hard. Burke was going to have to charge Jane with the accident knowing she was going to have a tough time realizing she had caused the death of her mother.

Upon arrival at the hospital, Burke was directed to room 201 and met with Jane and other family members. Jane had received numerous stitches to close wounds suffered during the accident. Jane then told Burke her side of the story.

Burke wrote Jane a traffic citation for improper left turn (causing an accident with death). Burke told Jane he was sorry to have to charge her. Burke did not charge her with traffic homicide, as he felt Jane would be suffering enough for the rest of her life.

"Blessed are those who mourn, for they shall be comforted." Matthew 5:4

CHAPTER 15

Dangerous Traffic Stop Ends Well

In the early morning hours, on this hot, clear, July night, Lt. Maurice Taylor stopped an old model dark colored 4 door Buick. The stop was on SR210, approximately 3 miles north of the town of Muckville. At 2:23 a.m. Lt. Taylor advised the midnight dispatcher, Tanya Young, he was making a traffic stop on the old dark colored Buick. He advised Young of his location and gave her the vehicle license tag number. He also advised that the vehicle was occupied by three males.

Sgt. Burke was only about three miles away and started heading toward Lt. Taylor. Burke turned on to SR210 and could observe the blue and red overhead lights on Taylor's patrol vehicle approximately one mile ahead. No other vehicles were on the road at this time. When Burke was approximately half a mile from Taylor, he turned off his headlights. As he arrived at the traffic stop area, at approximately 2:26 a.m., he parked on the right side of Taylor's patrol car which was located behind the stopped vehicle. Lt. Taylor was standing on the left side of his patrol vehicle, and the driver was standing in front of his vehicle. Lt. Taylor was starting to write the driver a citation.

Sgt. Burke exited his patrol car very quietly, and started to walk toward the stopped vehicle. Burke noticed the cars inside dome light was on. There was a passenger in the right front seat, and a passenger in the right rear seat. The passengers had apparently not noticed Sgt. Burke as he approached the vehicle. As Burke approached the area of the right rear door, he observed the long haired backseat passenger bend over and reach for a semi-automatic pistol located on the floor board. Burke reached through the open rear door window, grabbed the passenger by his hair, and pulled him out of the car, and yelled "gun!" to Lt. Taylor. Burke threw the passenger on the ground, looked up and observed Lt. Taylor with his service weapon pulled and pointed at the driver. Burke quickly handcuffed the suspect, then drew his service weapon and ordered the front seat passenger out of the vehicle, and also handcuffed him. By this time Lt. Taylor had cuffed the driver for his safety until they could figure out what was going on. Sgt. Burke also asked for two more deputies to respond to the scene.

Lt. Taylor advised Burke he had stopped the vehicle for unlawful speed, and the driver was James Anderson. The right rear passenger was Tom Wright, and the front seat passenger was Jake Scott. Burke then had Tanya run a NCIC/FCIC computer check on all three suspects.

As the officers were still at the scene trying to figure out what had transpired, Tanya advised Taylor and Burke that these three suspects had robbed a liquor store in the next county over, approximately an hour earlier. A witness had observed the three subjects running out of the liquor store, and obtained the tag number off the Buick. Tanya also advised that the two passengers, Tom Wright and Jake Scott, had also escaped from a North Florida prison, two days earlier.

All three subjects were transported to the county jail by Deputy Celina Adams, and Deputy Bobby Caruso. Burke and Taylor called for a tow truck to respond to the scene. They then searched the Buick. On the rear floorboard was a 45 caliber pistol. In the crack of the back seat was a bag of marijuana, and a large bag of cocaine. In the center console was a 9 mm pistol and another 9 mm pistol was found under the right front passenger seat. There were two-six packs of Budweiser beer on the right passenger seat floorboard.

The Buick was transported to the Sheriff's Office impound lot. Both Lt. Taylor and Sgt. Burke left the scene in route to the County Jail. At the jail the driver, James Anderson, was charged with unlawful speed, driving while license suspended, possession of cocaine, possession of marijuana, possession of a concealed firearm, armed robbery, and possession of a firearm during the commission of a felony. The two passengers, Tom Wright and Jake Scott, were charged with possession of marijuana, possession of cocaine, armed robbery, possession of a firearm during the commission of a felony, and escape from prison.

After the three were booked into the County Jail, Lt. Taylor and Sgt. Burke went to eat breakfast. It was while eating breakfast that Lt. Taylor realized that if Sgt. Burke had not arrived on the scene he probably would have been killed by Tom Wright, the back seat passenger. Sgt. Burke knew Taylor was right, but said "we both get to go home tonight. You have saved my neck a few times." Case closed by arrest.

Remember, God commissions angels to watch carefully over the lives and interests of the faithful. The angels were surely on duty this night.

"Rejoice always, pray without ceasing, and give thanks in all circumstances; for this is the will of God in Christ Jesus for you." 1 Thessalonians 5:16-18

CHAPTER 16

Cocaine Will Kill

Sgt. Burke was working the day shift on this October morning. Burke truly did not like working the day shift.

Sheriff Lance Rogers had a policy that each patrol Sergeant would inspect the patrol cars of each deputy on his shift, monthly. Sheriff Rogers wanted his patrol cars to be clean at all times, if possible. He also felt, the patrol car was the deputy's office, so the inside should be clean as well. When a patrol car got dirty, the deputy could drive behind the Sheriff's Department, and a trustee from the County Jail would wash it.

At approximately 9:00 a.m., Burke decided to start calling his shift deputies one at a time to meet him at different locations to start this month's inspections. It took several hours to complete this task. Burke would inspect the car for cleanliness, check the front driver and passenger seat area, back seat area, trunk, and then check the patrol cars maintenance record to make sure the deputies had their oil changed on time. He would also check the wear of the tires, etc.

Sgt. Burke then had lunch with Lt. Maurice Taylor at their favorite Bar-B-Que restaurant. Burke and Taylor discussed several problems going on with deputies on the shift. They decided to transfer two deputies to another assigned zone to separate them.

After lunch, Burke decided he would drive from the south end of the county, to the north end, on Highway 103, which runs all the way through Tomahawk County. This road has a reputation of being a drug corridor. Just north of the town of Garnet, Sgt. Burke clocked a red Chevy Camaro, on radar, at 81 miles per hour in a 55 mile per hour zone. The Camaro was traveling south on Highway 103. Burke turned his patrol car around, and activated his overhead red and blue lights, to stop the speeding vehicle. The red Camaro turned into the Renegade Hotel on the west side of Highway 103 just inside the city limits of Garnet. Burke advised the Sheriff's Department dispatcher, Summer, that he was 10-50 (stopping a vehicle) at the Renegade Hotel. He advised Summer of the description of the vehicle and the Florida tag number. The traffic stop occurred at 1:32 p.m.

As Sgt. Burke exited his patrol car, he observed the male driver bending over and moving around a lot. Burke became nervous due to all the movements being made by the driver. Burke asked the driver for his driver's license, vehicle registration, and insurance card. Burke then observed what he believed to be marijuana roaches (remnants of marijuana joints) in the ash tray of the center console. At this time Burke asked for Deputy Ethan Davis and K-9 Apache to be in route to his location at the Renegade Hotel.

Sgt. Burke asked the driver to stay in his vehicle, and Burke walked back to his patrol car and stood behind the right passenger door, and wrote the driver, Ray Lucas, a Florida traffic citation for unlawful speed. As Burke finished writing the citation, Deputy Davis and K-9 Apache arrived on the scene. Burke asked Deputy Davis to have Apache walk around the vehicle to conduct a narcotic search. K-9 Apache was a certified narcotic detection dog. At this time K-9 Apache began his search and soon alerted to the presence of drugs. Burke had Ray Lewis exit his vehicle and stand in front of Deputy Davis' patrol car, while Davis watched him. Deputy Davis advised Lucas that his dog had alerted to the vehicle which indicated the presence of drugs.

Burke then began his search of the vehicle. Five marijuana roaches were found inside the center console. In the glove compartment, Burke found two large zip lock baggies full of a green leafy substance that Burke believed to be marijuana as well. Burke told Lucas he was under arrest for possession of marijuana. Deputy Davis handcuffed Lucas. As Burke continued his search, he found a Smith & Wesson blue steel snub nose revolver under the driver's seat. Burke called in the serial number of the revolver, along with the make and model, to the dispatcher. Several minutes later, Summer advised Burke that the gun had been reported stolen as of a few months earlier (July). The revolver had been stolen during a burglary of a jewelry store in Garnet. Nothing else was found in the vehicle. The red Chevy Camaro was transported to the Tomahawk County Sheriff's Department impound lot by a local tow truck company.

Sgt. Burke transported Lucas to the County Jail. When he arrived at the jail, Lucas was staggering, and Burke needed help getting him inside the jail. Once inside the jail, Lucas was seated in a chair getting ready to be processed. A few minutes later, Lucas fell to the ground. EMS was called. Lucas began having convulsions and seizures and was foaming from his mouth. The ambulance arrived, and transported Lucas to the Seminole Memorial Hospital, in Seminole, some 15 miles away. Upon arrival at the hospital, he was pronounced dead.

An autopsy was performed the next day. During the autopsy, the county medical examiner found several small zip lock baggies in his stomach. They had been chewed up, and a white powdery substance was found throughout his stomach and in the baggies. This substance was believed to be cocaine. The medical examiner advised the results of the autopsy would be pending toxicology tests.

Two days later Burke received a call from Dr. Hook, the medical examiner. Hook stated Ray Lucas died of a drug overdose, from massive cocaine ingestion.

Sgt. Burke believed Lucas decided to eat, or swallow, the cocaine, sometime during the traffic stop instead of getting caught with the illegal drug. Case cleared by death of suspect.

"The waves of death surround me; the floods of destruction sweep over me. The grave wrapped its ropes around me; death itself stared me in the face." 2 Samuel 22:5-6

CHAPTER 17

Christmas Wrapped Present

Lt. Maurice Taylor, Sgt. Stoney Burke, and K-9 team Deputy Ethan Davis and Apache met with each other behind the Seminole Police Department on this cold afternoon, about a week before Christmas.

The three had decided they would patrol a major highway that runs through their county, Highway 103. This road had been a known drug corridor for several years, and numerous narcotic arrests had been made, and lots of marijuana and cocaine had been confiscated.

On this afternoon, Lt. Taylor and Sgt. Burke stopped several vehicles, and Deputy Davis had Apache conduct a narcotic search around the vehicles. No alerts and no narcotics had been found.

Lt. Taylor then stopped an older model four door beige Buick, on Highway 103, approximately five miles north of the town of Seminole. Lt. Taylor called in the traffic stop to Dispatcher Tanya. He gave her the location, description of the stopped vehicle, tag number, and told her the vehicle was occupied by a male driver and two female passengers.

After getting the vehicle stopped on the side of the road, he had the driver, later found to be Robert Williams, exit the car and walk back to the front of his patrol car. Sgt. Burke and the K-9 team pulled up and parked behind Lt. Taylor's patrol car. At this time Lt. Taylor started writing Williams a citation for unlawful speed. Sgt. Burke then walked up to the stopped vehicle and observed a bright colored Christmas wrapped box, sitting in the rear window area. Burke started a casual conversation with the two female passengers. During the conversation the passengers appeared extremely nervous, to Burke. They stated they were from Miami, heading to Georgia, for a family reunion. Burke then had Deputy Davis and K-9Apache conduct a narcotic search around the vehicle. While the K-9 team was conducting the narcotic search, Burke walked over to the area where Lt. Taylor and Robert Williams stood. Burke asked Williams where they were going. He answered by saying North Florida to a funeral. Sgt. Burke sensed something; very nervous passengers, conflicting stories.

K-9 Apache then made an alert to the rear of the vehicle which indicated the presence of drugs. Sgt. Burke asked the two passengers to exit the vehicle. They were found to be sisters; Ella and Louise Jones. Deputy Davis put Apache in the patrol vehicle and then watched the Jones sisters. Sgt. Burke began a vehicle search for drugs. Sgt. Burke opened the trunk and it was completely empty. No luggage or drugs. Sgt. Burke then began to search the interior of the vehicle to include the door panels, under the fire wall, under the seats, in the seat cushions, and no drugs were found. He then searched the hood area/engine compartment. Again, no drugs were found.

Sgt. Burke asked the Jones sisters what was inside the Christmas wrapped box in the back window. Louise Jones, who had been sitting in the back seat, stated it was a pair of blue jeans for her cousin for Christmas.

Sgt. Burke walked back to the vehicle and grabbed the box. The box was way too heavy for a pair of jeans. Since Apache had alerted on the vehicle and no drugs had been found, Burke decided to open the box. He found three packages wrapped in a clear tape. Burke knew from previous experience these were kilo (2.2 pounds) packages. He cut in to one package and observed a white powdery substance which he believed to be cocaine. Burke tested a sample from each package with a narcotic presumptive test kit. Each package came back positive for cocaine.

All three subjects were arrested and charged with possession of cocaine. The vehicle was towed from the scene. A total of $8,500 was confiscated from all three subjects. The packages of cocaine were weighed with the total weight being 6.7 pounds. This was a good Christmas gift to the Tomahawk County Sheriff's Department. Case closed by arrest.

Merry Christmas to all!

"If we deliberately keep on sinning after we have received the knowledge of the truth, no sacrifice for sin is left, but only a fearful expectation of judgement and of raging fire that will consume the enemies of God." Hebrews 10:26-27

CHAPTER 18

The Will to Live, or Not

The will to live is a psychological force for survival, seen as an important and active process of conscious and unconscious reasoning. This occurs particularly when one's own life is threatened by a serious injury or disease.

Sgt. Burke just finished lunch with Deputy Caruso, and they left the restaurant driving in opposite directions. Burke was going to the Sheriff's Office to gas up his patrol car, and have it washed.

At 1:38 p.m., Summer, the departments dispatcher, put out a call to Deputy Caruso, who was working the area of the county called Zone 4. Summer called by police radio, Tomahawk 36, which was Deputy Caruso's radio call number. Summer advised that a woman, who resides at 1010 Bowden Road, called in and stated her elderly male neighbor was walking around his yard with a long barreled weapon; either a rifle or shotgun. She stated the neighbors name was Ben Wilson, and he lived at 1013 Bowden Road. Tomahawk 36 advised Summer he would be 10-51 (in route) to the call which was located in a community of the county called Gatorview. Gatorview was located on Fairy Lane, about 2 miles south of Muckville. Sgt. Burke, Tomahawk 10, advised Summer that he was in route to the call as well. At 1:48 p.m. both Burke and Caruso arrived at 1013 Bowden Road, the residence of Ben Wilson. Burke advised Summer that he and Caruso were 10-97 (arrived at the call). When Burke and Caruso exited their patrol cars, Burke observed Ben Wilson walking back and forth in the screened in room on the front side of the residence. He still had the weapon in his hand. Both Burke and Caruso drew their service weapons, Beretta 40 caliber pistols, pointed them at Wilson and ordered him to drop his weapon. There was a very tense time when Wilson just stood there saying nothing, and not moving or doing what the deputies had ordered him to do. Burke was thinking to himself, please mister, drop your gun. I don't want to have to shoot you. Wilson had his weapon up and pointed towards the deputies. After six or seven times of being told to drop his weapon, Wilson finally complied with the officer's orders.

Burke and Caruso entered the screen room. Caruso took possession of the rifle. Burke then asked Mr. Wilson to step inside his house and they sat at the living room table. Wilson started to cry and stated he had cancer and was tired of all the pain, chemo, and radiation. Wilson stated he just wanted to end his life. He continued to state his wife Helen was gone to the store. He wanted to kill himself while she was gone.

At this time Wilson stood up and backed up three or four steps, turned, and ran toward a bedroom. Sgt. Burke jumped up and ran after him. Wilson jumped on his bed and shoved his hand under a pillow, and pulled out a revolver. Burke jumped on Wilson's back and grabbed the 357 magnum out of Wilson's right hand. Wilson continued to weep and stated, let me end it, let me end it. Burke then told Caruso to search the residence and confiscate every firearm that was located.

Burke decided to transport Wilson to the hospital for a 72-hour evaluation at the mental health department located there. Caruso found two revolvers, two shotguns, and three rifles, not counting the revolver Burke had taken away from Wilson. Caruso took the weapons to the Sheriff's Department for safe keeping. As Burke started to leave the residence with Ben Wilson, Ben's wife Helen pulled up into the driveway. Burke explained to Helen what had occurred and where Ben was going. Helen appeared to be mad, not worried, that we were taking Ben away.

Three days later Helen went to the Sheriff's Department and demanded to Sheriff Lance Rogers that her husband's weapons be returned to her. Helen stated she would give the guns to her son. Sheriff Rogers told the evidence custodian to get the confiscated weapons and place them in Helen Wilson's car. Helen then drove to the hospital and picked up Ben who had just been released, and they returned home. The next morning at 10:03 a.m. Summer called Sgt. Burke on the radio and advised him there had been a shooting at

1013 Bowden Road. Burke knew then exactly what had happened. Ben had committed suicide.

Sgt. Burke arrived at Wilson's house at 10:20 a.m. As he entered the house, Helen stated he had shot himself in the bedroom. Burke was extremely upset about the situation and thought to himself, "you can blame yourself lady, we told you not to bring the guns back home".

As Burke entered the bedroom, Ben was lying on the floor with his head facing south, with a bullet hole in his head. He was deceased. Investigation revealed that Ben laid on the floor, turned his head to the left, and holding in his right hand the same revolver taken out of his hands several days earlier, shot himself in the right side temple. The bullet went completely through his head and was found under the carpet and carpet padding in the cement floor. Tests were conducted on his right hand to determine if in fact he had recently fired a weapon. Test results were positive for gunshot residue which indicated he had fired his revolver.

Burke felt this was a needless death but probably would have happened one way or the other. Case closed by suicide.

"Therefore, I urge you, brothers, in view of God's mercy, to offer your bodies as living sacrifices, holy and pleasing to God, that this is your spiritual act of worship. Do not conform any longer to the pattern of this world, but be transformed by the renewing of your mind. Then you will be able to test and approve what God's will is – His good, pleasing, and perfect will." Romans 12:1-2

CHAPTER 19

Cocaine Kills, Again

On a Friday evening at approximately 11:15 p.m., Sgt. Burke and Lt. Maurice Taylor were attempting to stop a white Ford F-150 truck on Highway 103 for unlawful speed. A second vehicle, a red 4 door Toyota, interfered with their stop, nearly hitting Lt. Taylor's patrol car. Taylor and Burke then turned their attention to the second vehicle, the red Toyota. They were able to stop the vehicle on Highway 103, approximately 6 miles north of the town of Garnet. Burke called the traffic stop in to the Sheriff's Department dispatcher. He gave the description of the vehicle, tag number, location, and that it was occupied by two males.

When Taylor and Burke approached the vehicle, Taylor went to the driver's side and asked the driver to exit the vehicle. Burke went to the passenger's side. Both officers observed a white powdery substance on the center console. Burke also noticed the passenger making unusual movements. Burke then asked the passenger to exit the vehicle, which he did. When the passenger got out, Burke noticed what appeared to be crack cocaine and a white powdery substance on the passenger's seat. A narcotic presumptive test showed positive for the crack cocaine and white powder. By this time, other deputies had arrived on the scene for backup to assist if needed. Both subjects were placed under arrest for possession of cocaine. The passenger, Johnny Foreman, was transported to the county jail by Deputy Celina Adams, and the driver, James Woods, was transported to the jail by Deputy James Roe.

The passenger would not respond to questions, and did not speak. The driver told the officers at the time of arrest, that the passenger, Foreman, could not speak.

When Deputy Adams reached the county jail, she had to be assisted by Correction Officer Burns in getting Foreman into the jail. Foreman kept falling to the ground and kept his head down. When the handcuffs were removed inside the jail, Foreman fell to the ground on his face. As correctional officers rolled him over, Deputy Adams noticed a white substance coming from Foreman's mouth and he appeared to be chewing something. The officers attempted to remove the substance from his mouth, however, Foreman kept his jaws clenched. An ambulance was called, and the EMS personnel also attempted to remove the substance from his mouth. Foreman relaxed momentarily, and pieces of a plastic bag were removed from his mouth. By this time Sgt. Burke had arrived at the jail. Foreman continued to struggle with Sheriff's and EMT personnel until he passed out. The last thing he did before passing out was to hit an EMT in the nose with his fist and swing at a deputy.

Foreman was then transported to the Seminole Memorial Hospital with CPR being performed on the way, as well as after arriving at the hospital. Sgt. Burke followed the ambulance to the hospital. Foreman was pronounced dead at 2:06 a.m. early Saturday morning.

During this time the driver, James Woods, was booked into the Tomahawk County Jail and only spoke long enough to say that he wanted his attorney.

Burke believed Foreman had attempted to conceal cocaine hydrochloride and crack cocaine in his mouth. It appeared that one or more bags containing cocaine had broken and Foreman ingested a large amount of the substance.

Lt. Taylor and Sgt. Burke found 3 grams of crack cocaine loose, in and around the passenger seat of the vehicle.

An autopsy was performed later Saturday morning, and while no official cause of death had been released by the medical examiner, everything pointed to a cocaine related overdose.

Law enforcement officers in this area have been trying to get out the message that cocaine kills. This was the second cocaine death within a few months.

Both subjects were from Miami. James Woods, the driver, was charged with Possession of Cocaine, Trafficking in Cocaine and Possession of Marijuana under 20 grams. The marijuana had been found in Woods pants pocket. He was placed on $70,500 bond.

A week later the Sheriff's Office was contacted by the medical examiner's office in regards to Johnny Foreman's death. Cause of death was massive cocaine ingestion, which caused a heart attack. Case closed by one arrest, and one death.

"And God shall wipe away all tears from their eyes; and there shall be no more death, neither sorrow, nor crying, neither shall there be any more pain: for the former things are passed away." Revelation 21:4

CHAPTER 20

Party Ends with Tragedy

Late in the evening on a Friday night, a large group was having a party. The party was located at the extreme dead end of a dirt road known as Canal Road. This road was a dike which runs parallel to a canal.

Sgt. Burke had just started another night on the midnight shift, 11:00 p.m. to 7:00 a.m. Burke drove down Canal Road. He knew it was a hangout, party place, and just a place for people to meet. As Burke approached the dead end, he observed a bon fire, lots of vehicles, and a large group of about 30 to 40 young men and women. A lot of the partiers were observed drinking beer. Burke at random checked for IDs to determine if they were old enough to drink. It was not against the law to consume alcohol at that location. Burke knew from past experience that this group usually stayed and slept there until the next morning. Burke then talked to Juan Hernandez, who he had known for years. Burke told Hernandez before he continued his shift "no drinking and driving".

At approximately 12:05 a.m. Saturday morning Burke requested by police radio that all his zone deputies meet at Seminole Park, which was located in the middle of Tomahawk County. At approximately 12:20 a.m. all six of his deputies had arrived for a meeting with Burke. Burke discussed information that needed to be passed on to his deputies. He also discussed a pet peeve of his, while working the midnight shift. Burke stated, make sure you patrol your zone and check the businesses at least twice during the shift, especially just prior to the end of your shift. Burke believed it was better to find a burglary and call the owner, than for the owner to find it at 8:00 a.m. and call the Sheriff's Office. Sheriff Rogers did not like for a business owner to come to their business only to find the door smashed in or the entire plate glass window broken out. Burke ended the meeting and told his deputies to be safe.

At approximately 1:50 a.m., Tanya, the Sheriff's Department dispatcher called Sgt. Burke by police radio and advised him to meet Juan Hernandez at the end of Canal Road. Burke advised Tanya he would be in route to that location. When Burke arrived at the end of Canal Road he met with Juan. Juan stated his brother, Emanuel, and a friend, Edward Torres, had left the party area at approximately 11:40 p.m. to drive into Seminole to buy some more beer. They had not returned. Juan continued to state he had driven in to town looking for his brother, but could not locate him. Juan advised Burke his brother was driving a newer model black Dodge Ram truck. Burke told Juan to stay at the party area and make sure no one else left. Burke then broadcast the description of Emanuel's truck, told his deputies it had gone missing from Canal Road, and to let him know if they located it.

Burke left the party area and started looking down the canal road (the dike). By this time, it had started getting foggy and hard to see. After making several trips up and down Canal Road, Burke observed a faint set of tire tracks driving off the road. Burke exited his patrol car and followed the tire tracks down the edge of the dike and observed they had entered the canal. Burke could not see a vehicle, due to the dark water and fog. Burke firmly believed that this was Emanuel Hernandez's truck tires. It was now 3:18 a.m. Burke called Tanya and advised her of the situation, and asked her to call out members of the dive team to meet him on Canal Road, at daylight, approximately 6:30 a.m. Burke then called Major Ron Edwards, the Chief Deputy, at home and advised him what had occurred, what he was doing, and that he had called out the dive team. Major Edwards stated he would meet him at the scene at daylight.

Burke returned to the end of Canal Street where he advised Juan Hernandez of what he had found, and what was going to occur at daylight. Hernandez stated he would meet Burke at the location at daylight.

At daylight the dive team started to arrive on the scene. Sheriff Lance Rogers and Major Ron Edwards arrived on the scene together. Burke advised the dive team what he had found (the tire tracks leading in to the canal). The dive team put a small Jon boat with a 5 hp motor in the canal. Two divers got in the boat, and two divers entered the water at the spot the tire tracks entered the canal. Approximately 15 minutes later the divers in the water surfaced and stated they had discovered a Dodge truck down the canal approximately 30 yards from where it had entered the water. The divers stated the driver was still in the vehicle, seat belted in. Both front windows were open. Burke then had the dispatcher call a wrecker to the scene. When the wrecker arrived, the divers attached the winch to the truck in the canal. A black Dodge truck was pulled out. The body in the driver's seat was identified by Juan Hernandez as his brother, Emanuel Hernandez. Now we had to find Edward Torres. The divers reentered the water, down the canal from where the truck was located, due to the slight current. Approximately 45 minutes later, the divers found another body. It was that of Edward Torres, who was also identified by Juan Hernandez. The black Dodge truck was towed to the Sheriff's impound lot. The two bodies were transported by ambulance to the county morgue, located at Seminole Memorial Hospital. The next day an autopsy was performed on Emanuel Hernandez and Edward Torres. According to the medical examiner, both men died from drowning; alcohol related. Case closed by death.

"I am the resurrection and the life. He who believes in me will live, even though he dies; and whoever lives and believes in me will never die. Do you believe this?" John 11:25-26

CHAPTER 21

Sawed Off Shotgun
Robbery Spoiled

Deputy Celina Adams was working the afternoon shift in zone 3 of Tomahawk County. She was flagged down by a motorist at 9:55 p.m., 2 miles north of Seminole. The driver who flagged her down excitedly stated the following. He just drove by the Corner Store about a mile down the road. He observed a male exit a white Ford with what appeared to be a sawed off shotgun in his hands. Deputy Adams told the driver to please call the Sheriff's Department and give them his name and she would contact him later. She took off in route to the Corner Store. Adams also broadcast the information over the police radio to all deputies. The Corner Store was located on Highway 103. Adams was in route, traveling southbound on Highway 103. Sgt. Burke was headed north on Highway 103. As Burke arrived on the south side of the store, he observed a male run from the door of the store to a backed in, white, 4 door Ford. The Ford engine was running and a female was sitting in the driver's seat. The man jumped into the back seat carrying a sawed off shotgun. As Deputy Adams started pulling into the parking lot a shot rang out. Burke observed a barrel flash come from within the white Ford. Via police radio Burke asked Deputy Adams if she was okay and she replied yes. The white Ford took off at a high rate of speed. Burke was in pursuit with Deputy Adams following. Burke advised the dispatcher that he and Deputy Adams were 10-31 (in vehicle pursuit) and gave the direction of travel and the tag number on the vehicle. The dispatcher, Summer, then told Burke the tag was registered to a Roosevelt and Samantha Jones of 1112 East Golf Street, in the town of Garnett.

The officers were still in pursuit at a high rate of speed as the Ford turned right, eastbound, on to Elkins Drive. A second shot rang out from within the car. The shot missed both Burke and Adams and their vehicles. The pursuit continued. Two miles down the road the car turned south on to Davis Road. The Ford was traveling in excess of 100 miles per hour, according to Burke, as he continued to keep the dispatcher and other responding deputies up to date on the pursuit. Approximately 10 miles down Davis Road the white Ford failed to negotiate an extremely sharp curve in the road. The Ford slid off the road, the tires caught loose dirt and gravel, and due to the speed of the Ford, it flipped and overturned twice. It came to rest crashing into a large tree. Burke immediately reported the crash and requested an ambulance.

Burke and Adams exited their patrol cars and ran toward the Ford observing a small fire coming from the engine compartment. They continued to fear for their safety, since there was still the shotgun to be aware of. As the officers reached the car, a female later found to be Samantha Jones was strapped in by her seatbelt. She appeared to be okay but had several lacerations on her arms, legs, and face. Deputy Adams stayed with her while awaiting the arrival of an ambulance.

Sgt. Burke then noticed the male passenger was not in the vehicle. He also did not see the shotgun. The hairs on the back of his neck stood straight up. Oh lord! stated Burke. He drew his service weapon and with the use of his flashlight started a search for the passenger. Burke shortly discovered the passenger, identified as Roosevelt Jones. He was lying in the grass 20 feet from the Ford. Roosevelt was moaning and Burke could see he had a broken right arm and left leg. Roosevelt also had scratches and cuts all over his arms and face. Burke handcuffed Roosevelt as two ambulances arrived on the scene. Burke continued his search and recovered a sawed off shotgun approximately 15 feet from where Roosevelt was lying. Roosevelt had been ejected from the car, as it flipped and overturned several times. The back glass had been completely broken out.

EMT personnel worked on both subjects. Deputy Adams handcuffed Samantha Jones prior to the ambulances transporting both subjects to the hospital. Burke told Deputy Adams to stay at the scene and work the accident and call for a wrecker. Deputy Roe had arrived and helped Adams with traffic.

Sgt. Burke followed the ambulance to Seminole Memorial Hospital. At the hospital, Samantha was treated and released to Burke's custody. Roosevelt was handcuffed to a bed and treated for his injuries. According to the doctors, Roosevelt was going to be staying at the hospital for a while. Deputy Jim Burns had responded to the hospital at Burke's request and would be staying and guarding Roosevelt until relieved by another deputy.

Burke then transported Samantha to the county jail. She was charged with attempted robbery, fleeing and eluding police, and possession of marijuana that was found in her purse, as well as possession of a concealed firearm, also found in her purse.

Five days later, Roosevelt was released by the hospital and transported to the Tomahawk County Jail. Burke charged him with attempted armed robbery. On the evening of the attempted robbery, Roosevelt had walked into the Corner Store to rob it. As Burke pulled up, he fled. Roosevelt was also charged with aggravated assault with a firearm, shooting from within a vehicle, possession of a firearm during the commission of a felony, and most of all, possession of a short barreled shotgun. The barrel measured 12 inches. Burke was extremely thankful that neither he nor any of his deputies were injured on this night. Case closed by arrest.

"Do not trust in extortion, or take pride in stolen goods; though your riches increase, do not set your heart on them." Psalm 62:10

CHAPTER 22

Car Plunges into Canal

The Tomahawk County Sheriff's Department is located in the town of Seminole, the County Seat. The department is on Justice Way near the intersection of Fish Highway. Justice Way is a very busy road, especially early in the morning and late afternoon. Across Justice Way is a large canal that runs parallel to the road.

It was a beautiful, sunny, bright spring morning, and as usual there was a lot of traffic on Justice Way. Sgt. Burke, along with other patrol supervisors, was in a meeting with Major Ron Edwards, the Chief Deputy.

At approximately 9:18 a.m. Burke exited the Sheriff's Office and started to enter his patrol vehicle. Burke heard tires squealing and a loud crash sound. He looked up and observed a dark colored car plunge into the canal near the intersection of Fisher Highway. Burke observed another vehicle spin around and stop near the intersection. Burke quickly called in the crash, by radio, and requested the fire department and an ambulance.

Sgt. Burke ran across the street and observed a man in the water. The man apparently could not swim, and went under water two or three times. Burke dove into the canal, as the man sank under the dark murky water. Burke pulled the man up and got him to the canal bank where several firemen helped pull him out of the water. Deputy Eddie Raulerson, who was in the Sheriff's Department parking lot, drove over and heard people saying they believed someone else was in the car. Both Burke and Raulerson made several dives down to the car, in about 10 feet of water. The man that had been pulled from the canal then stated, no one else was in the vehicle. The driver was identified as Hector Sequndo. The EMTs that arrived on the scene checked Hector and he appeared to be okay.

Burke then asked for a tow truck to respond to the crash site. Burke told Deputy Raulerson to work the accident, then go home to change his clothes.

When the tow truck arrived, Burke took the hook at the end of the tow truck winch, and reentered the water. Burke dove down and hooked the winch to the bottom of the submerged car. The car was pulled out of the canal where Deputy Raulerson took photos and got the information on the car for his crash report.

Burke then went home to change his uniform, after which, he returned to the crash site and spoke to Raulerson. Investigation revealed that Hector Sequndo had run a red light at the intersection, hit another vehicle, and drove into the canal, after losing control of his car. Both vehicles had heavy damage. The elderly driver of the other car did not appear to be injured, but Deputy Raulerson talked him in to going to the hospital by ambulance to be checked out. Sequndo's vehicle was towed to the wrecker service impound lot.

Deputy Raulerson charged Hector Sequndo with causing the accident. He was charged with running a red light, and careless driving. Investigation also revealed Sequndo was traveling approximately 30 miles per hour over the posted speed limit.

Deputy Raulerson finally got the opportunity to go home and change his uniform. Sgt. Burke asked Raulerson to meet him for lunch at the local Bar B Que restaurant at 11:15 a.m. During lunch, Sgt. Burke told Raulerson, a young rookie, he did a great job. Burke even paid for his lunch.

After lunch Burke told Deputy Raulerson to go to work and "earn your money". Of course Burke was kidding. Both officers left the restaurant wondering what the rest of the day would bring. Burke thanked God that no one was injured in the crash.

"The Lord will keep you from all evil; He will keep your life. The Lord will keep your going out and your coming in from this time." Psalm 12:7-8

CHAPTER 23

Stupid Things People Do

During the mid-morning hours, Gator Adams was driving his older model beige colored VW Beetle in the town of Garnet, on Hammock Road. Sgt. Burke just happened to pull up beside Gator's VW at a red light. Burke looked over and observed a plant sitting on the back seat. Burke stated to himself "that's not a marijuana plant!" Burke looked again and answered his own question. "Yes, it is a marijuana plant!"

Burke let Gator take off from the light and pulled in behind him. Burke knew Gator from some previous encounters, all of which were drug related. Burke activated his overhead red and blue lights and advised the dispatcher he would be making a traffic stop on Hammock Road and Dell Avenue, on an old beige VW Beetle, and he gave her the Florida tag number.

As Burke walked up to Gator's VW he observed the marijuana plant was approximately 3 feet tall. Burke asked Gator for his driver's license, registration, and insurance card. Gator fumbled through his wallet and finally handed his Florida driver's license to Burke.

Burke asked Gator what kind of plant that was on the back seat. Gator replied "you know what it is; a marijuana plant." Burke asked Gator to exit his car and advised him he was under arrest for possession of marijuana. Burke then cuffed Gator and advised him of his Miranda rights. Gator stated he understood his rights. He was placed in the back seat of Burke's patrol car.

Burke searched the VW and found a large zip lock bag full of a green leafy substance, that again, looked like marijuana. A narcotic presumptive test revealed the substance to be marijuana, which weighed approximately one pound.

Burke knew Gator had a criminal record. Gator was asked where he got the plant and the pound of marijuana. Gator surprisingly told Burke he had purchased everything from Phillip Simmons who lives out on Parrish Ranch Road. Gator stated he had just purchased the marijuana. Gator further stated that Simmons had a greenhouse behind his residence and he saw approximately 80-100 marijuana plants and observed lots of baggies of marijuana sitting on the table in the greenhouse.

Gator's VW was towed and impounded at the Sheriff's Office impound lot. Burke then transported Gator to the county jail at which time he stated he would help us any way he could. After booking Gator into the county jail, Burke met with Captain Bob Evans, the narcotic division supervisor. Burke advised Captain Evans of the information relayed by Gator.

At Captain Evans request, Burke filled out an application and affidavit for a search warrant on Phillip Simmons property, house, and greenhouse. Burke then took the search warrant to the office of Judge Joe Rogers to get the judge to sign the warrant. Judge Rogers grew up with Burke and became a lawyer. He was now the County Judge.

Captain Evans gathered several narcotic agents, along with Sgt. Burke. Late in the afternoon, the officers served a search warrant at Phillip Simmons residence, greenhouse, cars, and property. Agents found 87 marijuana plants, all averaging 3 feet tall; 30 – 1-pound zip lock baggies of marijuana; $9,000 in cash; and a sawed off shotgun, in the greenhouse. No drugs were found in the cars, or the Simmons residence.

Simmons was arrested for possession of marijuana with intent to sell, cultivation of marijuana, and possession of a short barreled shotgun. Case cleared by arrest.

"Do not be deceived; bad company ruins good morals."
1 Corinthians 15:33

CHAPTER 24

Some Good Leisure Time on Patrol

Every month or so, Sgt. Burke would pick a night for some leisure time. Burke would pick a night when his crew was working the graveyard shift. Burke would tell his deputies to BYOS to work. That's bring your own steak.

This Thursday night was a BYOS night. The evening would start with a 10:45 p.m. shift change briefing. Burke would tell his deputies to go out and patrol their assigned zones really good, and meet at the club house at 12:30 a.m. Deputies then started their shift.

Sgt. Burke headed to the clubhouse (Sheriff's clubhouse/ range). Burke would start the charcoal in the grill, and start a large pot of water to boil. He would then go to one of the packing houses in the area and get some good sweet corn, for corn on the cob. Burke then started patrolling the county.

At approximately 12:30 a.m., if the deputies were not on a call, they would meet at the clubhouse. They would boil corn and grill steaks. They would sit down, say a prayer, and enjoy a good grilled steak and corn on the cob.

Now the trouble starts; having to continue the shift on a very full stomach. The deputies would leave and return to their assigned zones. Burke would lock up the clubhouse and shooting range gate, and return to his supervisor duties.

At approximately 2:20 p.m. Sgt. Burke advised Tanya, the department's dispatcher, he would be out of his patrol car on foot at a large strip mall on Highway 103, just south of Seminole. Burke walked the front side of the mall checking doors and windows for possible burglaries. Burke then walked to the rear, still looking for possible burglaries. Burke stopped and was looking around the area. As he stood with his back to one of the business doors, he heard the door behind him start to open. Burke pulled his service weapon, then saw a hand coming out on the far side of the door holding a screwdriver. As a man stepped outside, Burke put his service weapon to the man's head, and stated "Sheriff's Department, drop the screwdriver". The man turned his head and was looking down the barrel of a Beretta 40 caliber pistol. The man immediately dropped the screwdriver and lay on the ground, face down, as ordered by Burke. He was known by Burke as Mike Anderson, a known thug, burglar, and druggie. He was handcuffed at that time, and then searched. In his left rear pocket there was a white envelope containing $600. Deputy Celina Adams had responded to the scene as requested by Burke. Adams transported Anderson to the County Jail. Burke then searched the inside of the deli for other suspects.

Sgt. Burke had the dispatcher contact the owner of the deli by phone and asked them to come to the deli. Several minutes later, Tanya told Burke that Louie O'Malley and his son Antonio would be responding to the scene. Approximately 35 minutes later, the O'Malley's arrived at the back door to the deli. Burke asked them to search the deli to see if anything had been stolen. Louie O'Malley told Burke that an envelope with $600 was missing. The envelope had the name of the deli on it (Louie's Deli). Burke then looked closely at the envelope full of money taken from Mike Anderson. It had Louie's Deli printed on it. Burke took a photo of the envelope containing the money and returned it to Louie. Antonio O'Malley then told Burke that the suspect had eaten a sandwich and drank a coke. Burke jokingly stated "I guess you'll have to charge him".

Sgt. Burke then looked around the deli to determine how the suspect, Mike Anderson, made entry. Burke discovered the point of entry was a low bathroom window, which had been jimmied, located on the back side of the business. Louie O'Malley advised Burke he was going to have bars installed on the windows to prevent any further burglaries. Burke advised Louie that would be an excellent idea. Burke then left and drove to the county jail. At the jail, Burke talked to Mike Anderson. Anderson was read his Miranda rights. Anderson then wrote out a complete confession about the full deli burglary. Anderson told Burke he was a drug addict and needed money for drugs. Anderson told Burke he needed help, and wanted to get off drugs. Burke then told Anderson he would give him some information about different rehab programs. Anderson continued to state his parents would help financially if he would get off the drugs. Burke told Anderson that was great, and he hoped he would follow through with a rehab program.

Anderson was booked into the jail and charged with burglary and grand theft. Case closed by arrest.

Sgt. Burke left the jail and minutes later responded to assist another deputy with a possible DUI traffic stop.

"Ye shall not steal, neither deal falsely, neither lie one to another." Leviticus 19:11

CHAPTER 25

Murderer Apprehended

Another graveyard shift started on this cool winter December night. It appeared to Sgt. Stoney Burke it was going to be a slow night, as many others were.

At 1:18 a.m. Dispatcher Tanya put out a BOLO (be on lookout) for a white Chevy Z-71 truck with a Florida tag. The truck was last seen driven by a male named Jesse Maxwell. Maxwell was being sought for a murder that had just occurred at a beach bar several counties away. According to Tanya, the murder had been witnessed by several subjects in the parking lot of the bar. According to some witnesses, Maxwell used a 30/30 rifle to commit the murder. Tanya advised the deputies that Maxwell resided in Tomahawk County. His truck license tag came back to an address of 3333 Florida Avenue, in the town of Cherokee.

Burke knew if Maxwell was coming home from the beach there were only 3 possible roads to take, unless he drove way out of his way. At that time Burke told Deputy Ethan Davis and Apache to patrol Highway 291; Deputy John Earl was told to patrol the old Indian Highway. He then told Deputy Adams to go and park in an area to observe the entrance into the residential area where Maxwell lived. Burke told Deputy Caruso to stay in the area of Cherokee. Sgt. Burke then decided to drive out on the lonely Highway 404. He drove out approximately 19 miles and parked in the parking lot of a closed Tom Thumb store. This store was just about a mile from the county line.

At 2:38 a.m. a white Chevy Z-71 truck drove west bound on Highway 404 and passed Sgt. Burke's location. Burke pulled in behind the truck to verify the license tag number. It matched, so Burke radioed in that he was behind the suspect's truck heading toward Cherokee. Burke began to direct his deputies to set up a road block at an intersection just about a mile from Cherokee. Burke continued to follow Maxwell at a slight distance, as deputies hurried to get in place to stop Maxwell at the roadblock location.

Maxwell started slowing down, but continued driving westbound. Maxwell got slower, and Burke told two of the deputies to start heading his way for backup.

Maxwell then stopped his truck in the middle of the road, and Burke radioed in the information to the responding deputies. Burke began to have anal contractions, and he knew it was probably going to be a bad situation, knowing Maxwell had just murdered someone and he was armed with at least a known 30/30 rifle.

Burke stopped his patrol car, turned on his red and blue lights, and pointed a spotlight to shine into the interior of the stopped truck. Burke stood behind his open patrol car door, armed with this 12-gauge shotgun, loaded with buckshot. Burke ordered Maxwell to turn off his truck, which he did not. Burke ordered Maxwell to open his door from the outside handle and to exit his truck. Maxwell refused these orders. Burke could hear his deputies responding to his location with sirens blaring. Burke then saw the blue lights of his deputies at a far, far, distance. At this time, Burke observed Maxwell making all kind of movements within his truck. Burke decided to walk around the rear of his patrol car and approach Maxwell's truck from the passenger side. Burke hoped Maxwell could not see him, due to the spotlight shining into the truck. As Burke approached the passenger door, he noticed the passenger door window was open. He could see Maxwell sitting there, holding the 30/30 on his lap with the barrel facing the driver's door. Maxwell was looking out the driver's window. Burke stuck his shotgun into the open passenger window and pointed it at Maxwell's head. Burke ordered Maxwell to hand the rifle to him through the window, butt first. Maxwell did as ordered and Burke grabbed the rifle and threw it on the ground as other deputies arrived. Sgt. Burke held his shotgun on Maxwell as Deputy Caruso got him out of the truck and handcuffed him.

Burke searched the truck but found no other weapons. Burke transported Maxwell to the County Jail where he was booked in and charged with murder. Tanya contacted the other county and advised them that the Tomahawk County Sheriff's Department had arrested Jesse Maxwell on their murder charge. Case cleared by arrest.

Sgt. Stoney Burke received a letter of commendation from Sheriff Lance Rogers for exemplary performance as a Deputy Sheriff (aiding in the apprehension of a murder suspect).

"Ye have heard that it was said by them of old time, thou shall not kill; and whosoever shall kill be endangered of the judgment." Matthew 5:21

CHAPTER 26

Traffic Stop Nets 26 Pounds of Cocaine

Seminole Police Sgt. Tom Hill and Officer Brian Griffin made a routine traffic stop on Highway 103. Sgt. Hill stopped a 1982 Buick Limited for unlawful speed. The vehicle was traveling 69 miles per hour in a 45 mile per hour zone. Officer Griffin responded as a backup.

Sgt. Hill asked the driver for his driver's license. The driver fumbled through his wallet and appeared to be extremely nervous. After Hill obtained the driver's license he identified the driver as Morales Rolando, from Miami Florida. Sgt. Hill told Rolando he had stopped him for unlawful speed and asked him to exit his vehicle and walk to the front of Hill's patrol car.

Prior to writing Rolando a Florida traffic citation, for the unlawful speed violation, he engaged Rolando in casual conversation. During this conversation, Rolando told Hill he was traveling north to Georgia to attend a family reunion.

Hill noticed that Rolando still appeared to be extremely nervous and had started to sweat profusely.

Sgt. Hill asked his dispatcher to call the Sheriff's Office and request a K-9 unit, if close and available.

Tanya, the Sheriff's dispatcher then radioed Deputy Ethan Davis and K-9 Apache, and requested he respond to the location of Sgt. Tom Hill's traffic stop in Seminole. Deputy Davis told Tanya he would be 10-51 (in route) to Sgt. Hill's location.

Sgt. Burke and Lt. Maurice Taylor were talking to Sheriff Lance Rogers in the parking lot of the Sheriff's Department. The Sheriff was heading home.

Sgt. Burke and Lt. Taylor decided to drive down to watch their K-9 team conduct the narcotic search. At 5:28 p.m. Deputy Sheriff Davis and Apache arrived at the scene of the traffic stop. Burke and Taylor arrived a minute later. Sgt. Hill asked Deputy Davis if he would have K-9 Apache conduct a narcotic search around Rolando's car. Hill suspected there may be drugs inside the car.

Deputy Davis retrieved Apache from his car, put him on a leash, and walked him to the front of the stopped car and gave him the command "find the dope". Apache started sniffing the exterior of the car, walking in a counter clockwise direction around the car. When Apache reached the trunk area, he became aggressive and started scratching and biting at the trunk. That was Apache's alert that he had smelled the presence of a narcotic that he had been trained to detect. Deputy Davis praised Apache for a good job, and placed him back in his patrol car.

Deputy Davis then told Sgt. Hill the dog had alerted. Deputy Davis asked Rolando if he understood English. Rolando replied "yes". Davis told Rolando that his dog, Apache, was a certified narcotic detection dog. He had alerted to the vehicle and the officers were going to search it.

Seminole Police Sgt. Hill, and Officer Brian Griffin, searched the entire car and found no drugs. Sgt. Hill also pointed out that Rolando had told him he was going to Georgia to attend a family reunion. There was no luggage or other clothing found in the car.

Deputy Davis then placed Apache inside the car to conduct another narcotic search. Apache again alerted. This time it was on the back part of both driver and passenger seats. Deputy Davis placed Apache back in his patrol car.

Sgt. Hill and Sgt. Burke then started to search the inside of the vehicle. Sgt. Burke observed a zipper running down the upholstery of the seats. Burke unzipped the zipper and upon reaching inside the seat back, discovered packages wrapped in tape. From experience, he knew this was a common way of wrapping cocaine. Burke started to pull out the packages. He also knew, from experience, that each package was one kilo, 2.2 pounds. Burke pulled out 6 packages from each seat. Each package was field tested with a narcotic presumptive test. Test results were positive for cocaine. The 12 packages had a total weight of 26.4 pounds of cocaine.

The officers continued to search the vehicle for additional narcotics. They tore out the glove compartment, pulled out the center console, and pulled off the inside door panels of all 4 doors. They pulled out the back seat and checked under the car for any possible secret compartments. No other narcotics were found. Sgt. Burke was extremely pleased and excited about the job Deputy Davis and Apache had done. Especially because Burke used to be K-9 Apache's handler.

Rolando was transported to the Tomahawk Count Jail by Sgt. Hill. At the jail, through a computer check, Hill discovered that Rolando's driver's license was also suspended. Rolando was charged with Possession of Cocaine, Trafficking in Cocaine, Unlawful Speed, and Driving While License Suspended. Bond was set at $500,000.

The Seminole Police Department would be continuing their investigation in reference to this narcotic arrest. The car had a Michigan tag on it. The owner was not known at this time. Rolando told officers that someone had given him the car to use and told him to leave it somewhere in Georgia. Rolando was given $4,000 by an unknown subject for driving the car and getting himself home. The money was confiscated and placed in evidence.

Sgt. Burke told news reporters that "every gram we get, is a gram that doesn't get on the streets". Case cleared by arrest.

"Be sober-minded; be watchful. Your adversary, the devil, prowls like a roaring lion, seeking someone to devour." 1 Peter 5:8

CHAPTER 27

Caught in Pot Field

On the north side of Tomahawk County, there is a large community called Lake Sumter. Lake Sumter is a great fishing spot with several fish camps and a small town area with numerous businesses, stores, gas stations, a bank and a restaurant.

In the community, there was a family by the name of Weaver, who ran a junk yard about a mile from the lake, with lots of woods surrounding the residence, and junk yard. The Weavers had three sons, named James, John, and Jeb. They were all bad boys and were in and out of trouble. One day, Deputy Sheriff Caruso was patrolling in the Lake Sumter area. He was stopped by a person that Caruso had known for several years. We will call him Todd. Todd told Deputy Caruso that the Weaver boys were growing marijuana, which was no big surprise to Caruso. Todd continued to state the Weaver's pot field was located in the woods, approximately one mile south of the Weaver's junk yard. It was on the north side of Fish Lane Road, near the old closed down gas station. Several hours later Deputy Caruso went to the

Sheriff's Office and met with Sgt. Burke and Captain Bob Evans, the narcotic division supervisor. Deputy Caruso told both supervisors of the information he had received from his snitch, Todd. Captain Evans told Burke and Caruso he had received information that the Weaver boys were growing marijuana, however, he did not know the exact location.

Captain Evans did not want to use an undercover narcotic agent to go find the marijuana field. He did not want to take the chance someone would see him and bust his cover. Captain Evans asked Sgt. Burke if he could use Caruso to search the woods in an attempt to locate the pot field. Sgt. Burke agreed and Captain Evans met with Sheriff Rogers to let him know of the plans and get the Sheriff's approval.

Several days later, the plans were set in motion. Deputy Caruso would drive to an area near the old closed down gas station in his personal truck. Lots of people parked in that area to fish up and down the nearby canal leading to the lake. Sgt. Burke and Deputy Ethan Davis and Apache would be in the Lake Sumter area if needed as backup.

About an hour later Deputy Caruso found the pot field. At first glance it appeared to contain approximately 90 marijuana plants. Caruso also noticed numerous one-gallon water jugs; some full and some empty. As Caruso continued to sneak around the pot field looking for possible booby traps, he heard a noise. When he looked up he observed James Weaver walking to the pot field carrying jugs of water. As the two met eyes, James Weaver yelled "hey, what are you doing here!?" And he ran towards Caruso.

James Weaver grabbed Caruso around the neck and Caruso identified himself as a Deputy Sheriff. James stated he did not care who he was. The two struggled for several minutes. Caruso was trying to get James on the ground and under control to handcuff him. James then broke loose and took off running north through the woods. Deputy Caruso stayed and radioed Sgt. Burke and Deputy Davis of the situation. Sgt. Burke advised Caruso they were in route to his location. When the officers arrived at the old gas station, Caruso talked them into his location by giving directions over the radio.

When Burke and Davis arrived at Caruso's location he told them exactly what had occurred. Caruso showed Davis where he last observed James Weaver running. Davis took K-9 Apache to that area and Apache soon took off on James Weaver's trail. Approximately 20 yards into the track, Apache stopped. Deputy Davis looked down and saw a brown wallet. Davis opened the wallet and it contained the driver's license of James Weaver. K-9 Apache then continued his track with Sgt. Burke and Deputy Caruso following behind the K-9 team. The track turned and continued toward the Weaver house. The officer's also walked up on an old 3-wheeler, believed to belong to the Weavers. The track continued toward the Weaver property. The officers stopped their track at the driveway near the Weaver's wood privacy fence gate. The officers then returned to the pot field, photographed the area, and pulled all the marijuana plants which numbered 98. All plants were approximately 5 feet tall. Sgt. Burke then asked that Deputy John Earl respond to the scene in his patrol truck. Burke told Earl to go by the Sheriff's Office on his way and pick up their large covered trailer. The officers also confiscated the abandoned 3-wheeler. After all the plants were pulled up and loaded in the trailer, they returned to their cars at the gas station. Deputy Earl transported the marijuana to the Sheriff's Office in the trailer.

Sgt. Burke, Deputy Caruso, and the K-9 team departed in route to the Weaver residence. When the officers arrived they observed James on the front porch. They arrested him, and as they were attempting to handcuff him, brothers John and Jeb jumped on Deputy Caruso, saying you ain't taking him to jail. As John and Jeb started to hit and kick Caruso, Sgt. Burke grabbed John and pulled him off. K-9 Apache grabbed Jeb. Fight over, and three arrested. The Weaver boy's parents were not home at the time. Sgt. Burke left a note on the front porch with his business card. Note read "all three boys in jail".

The three Weaver boys were transported to the County Jail by Sgt. Burke. On the way to the jail Jeb asked "how did you find our pot"? Burke replied "good police work". The boys were all booked under the following charges; Cultivation of Marijuana, Battery on a Law Enforcement Officer, and Resisting Arrest with Violence.

Burke then met with Deputies Earl, Caruso, and Davis. They all unloaded the marijuana, photographed the plants again, and assisted the evidence custodian in placing the marijuana in the evidence room. Captain Evans and Sheriff Rogers met the officers in the evidence room and congratulated them for a great job. Case closed by arrest.

"The Lord saw that the wickedness of man was great in the earth, and that every intention of the thoughts of his heart was only evil continually." Genesis 6:5

CHAPTER 28

Officer Pranks

Sgt. Burke left the Sheriff's Office after the 10:45 p.m. shift change, to start another graveyard shift. It was raining hard. Burke stated this is definitely a frog strangler. As time passed the rain got worse. There was hardly a car on the road and there had been no calls to respond to. It was extremely quiet throughout the entire county.

Sgt. Burke drove out to Lake Sumter and parked at a small park. He sat back and began to reminisce about 13 years back when he was just a young deputy way too full of himself. He thought about some of the funny pranks the deputies played on one another.

Snake

Burke was just a young Deputy working on the afternoon shift under a Sergeant named Roy Williams. All the deputies knew that Williams was extremely scared of snakes. One afternoon one of the deputies caught a four-foot rat snake and placed it in a pillow case. He arrived at roll call early on this particular day, took the snake out of the pillow case and placed it in Sgt. Williams top desk drawer. We all knew that when the Sergeant came in for roll call he would open his desk and pull out a legal sized pad of paper for writing down information. All the deputies were present and waiting for the Sergeant to arrive to start shift change.

Sgt. Williams entered the room, sat down, and talked briefly to several of the deputies. Williams then reached for his desk drawer. We were all eyes and about to bust a gut laughing. As Williams opened the drawer the snake sprung out quickly. The Sergeant jumped straight up and yelled "Oh my god" and drew his service weapon. It looked like Williams sprung up about 3 feet. All the deputies hit the floor laughing. As we looked at Williams he was dancing around, as the snake was now on the floor. We thought the he was going to shoot the snake. He was very scared. When all settled down, the Sergeant laughed and said "pay backs are going to be rough, boys". The snake was caught, taken outside and released. We finished shift change and went to work.

Sgt. Williams is now deceased. I think of him often. I learned a lot from this man, as a young deputy.

The Skeleton

Another time for fun. Our day shift had just ended and we would be off for several days. One of our deputy's fathers owned a vault company near the airport. On the side of this business was a pile of old metal caskets. They were believed to have been used to carry deceased soldiers back home from the war.

During the last two weekends on a Friday night several caskets had been stolen. Burke and two other deputies, one being the son of the vault company owner, got permission to set up surveillance at the business.

The next day was Friday. We met at noon at the vault company. We moved some caskets around to make them easier to grab and load on to a truck. We planned for Burke to get on the roof of the building. The owner's son would lie down in the top casket with a skeleton mask on. The third deputy would be in his personal truck parked just down the road. We left the vault company and agreed to meet back at 10:00 p.m.

At 10:00 p.m. sharp we met and assumed our positions. It was a cool night so the deputy inside the casket would not be too uncomfortable. We were equipped with walkie talkies which had earphones so we could talk and the sound wouldn't broadcast for others to hear. At 11:48 p.m. Burke observed an old dark colored truck slowly coming down the road without its headlights on. It drove around the area and returned to the side of the vault company. Burke alerted the two deputies about what was going on. The man exited the truck and walked over to the area of the caskets. Burke told the deputy inside the casket to be ready. The man moved one casket over, then opened the baited casket. The deputy wearing the skeleton mask yelled and jumped up as the man opened the lid. The man yelled and took off running down the road, leaving his truck where it was parked. The deputy in his personal truck, pulled out and got the man to stop.

He was scared to death, and the deputies were quite sure this may have turned this man's life around.

The Lost Television

Burke was working midnights. During roll call Burke was told that a Lt. from another shift, Lt. Spencer, would be working an off duty security detail at a construction site. Lt. Spencer was an elderly man about to retire. The construction site was located in the zone that Burke was assigned to work. Actually it was located on the line between two zones. Burke knew from previous occasions the Lt. would take a small television and watch it while on his security detail. He also knew that Lt Spencer would sometimes fall asleep. The plot thickens. Burke has a plan.

At approximately 2:10 a.m. Burke and Deputy John Tucker met near the construction site. With binoculars, they could see Lt. Spencer sitting in his patrol car and he appeared to be asleep. Burke noticed a television sitting on the hood near the windshield in front of the driver's seat. A power plug ran to the car, apparently plugged in to the cigarette lighter.

As previously planned Deputy Tucker had tied numerous empty cans to a thin rope. The rope was approximately 10 feet long. Burke and Tucker snuck down to Lt. Spencer's car. Tucker gently tied one end of the rope to the back of Spencer's car. Burke unplugged the television power cord, leaving it plugged in to the cigarette lighter. Burke removed the television and both deputies left the area with it. They drove off in separate directions.

Lt. Spencer woke up about 35 minutes later only to notice his television had been taken. Spencer got on the radio and demanded to know who had taken his television. No one answered back. He then demanded that his television be returned. Still, no one admitted taking it. At 7:00 a.m. Lt. Spencer cranked up his car and started to drive away and go home. Then came the clanking of the cans as he drove. He slammed on brakes, got out of the car, and found the cans. He was really furious by now.

Spencer got on the radio and told all the midnight shift deputies to meet him at his office immediately. All the deputies arrived and Lt. Spencer raked them over the coals. But no one would tell what happened to the television. Burke had taken the television and placed it on the hood of Lt. Spencer's private car at his residence. No one ever told Spencer who had stolen his television.

Lt. Spencer later retired, and is now deceased. We had lots of laughs over the years playing pranks on each other.

We are to give thanks in the good times, because giving thanks makes us appreciate what we have been given. A person who is always complaining and never grateful is a person who does not know the riches of life. We have taken the time to count our blessings, when we make it a point to focus on the wonderful things we have been given. We appreciate life more.

CHAPTER 29

Back Talk to Deputy Lands Date with Judge

Sgt. Burke got up extra early and drove down to one of his favorite restaurants in Muckville for breakfast, prior to going to roll call for the day shift. As Burke ate breakfast, he sat down at the table, called the liars table. Businessmen, mostly older, retired men, who ate there every morning sat at this table. Sheriff Lance Rogers also came in and had breakfast. He sat next to Sgt. Burke. During breakfast, Sheriff Rogers, who was in an extremely good mood, stated as he patted Burke on the back "here is a future sheriff". Burke did not know what to say. However, he told the Sheriff thank you very much. I hope I can be half the Sheriff you have been.

Burke left the restaurant to drive to the Sheriff's Office for shift change. After a brief meeting with his deputies, and assigning them their work zones, Burke started to drive around the county. He drove to the north end, and stopped and talked to several business owners. He stopped at several fish camps to see if the fish were biting. Burke loved to go fishing. He then slowly started making his way southbound. At around 10:53 a.m. Sgt. Burke drove in to Muckville and took several turns where numerous bars were located. As Burke approached the Jackson Bar, he noticed a black male staggering in the street and waving his arms around as if he were directing traffic. Burke stopped his patrol car, got out, and approached the man later found to be Ray Campbell. Burke told Campbell to get out of the road and go home or he would be arrested. Another unknown male walked over and grabbed Campbell by the arm and stated "Mr. Stoney, I'll get him home, don't arrest him". Burke said that would be a great idea. I don't want to have to arrest him. Burke could smell alcoholic beverages on Campbell as he talked trash. He smelled like he had not bathed in a week or so. Campbell also gave Burke instructions as to where he could kiss him, as he walked away toward the bar with the other unknown man. Burke just smiled and got in to his patrol car.

Burke then drove down the road and talked to a man that was a witness to a burglary a few days earlier. The burglary occurred in the north end of the county. This man, Mr. Lewis Shelton, was fishing and observed someone break in to a mobile home.

After the conversation with Mr. Lewis, Burke drove back toward the Jackson Bar in route to Highway 103. Again he observed Ray Campbell in the middle of the street under a traffic light. Campbell was staggering as he attempted to walk, and was again directing traffic. He almost got hit by several cars. He would use his hand to bang the hoods of cars as they passed. Burke stopped in the intersection and activated his red and blue lights. Burke exited his car and heard Campbell talking in a loud and disorderly manner. Burke warned Campbell to stop his loud and boisterous talk, and stop cussing. Campbell then said "go ahead, you sorry pig, put me in jail". He then stated "you are not man enough to arrest me and put me in your car". Burke was finally tired of Campbell's actions. He was extremely intoxicated, and was not going home to sleep it off.

Burke grabbed Campbell by his left arm and told him he was under arrest for disorderly intoxication. Campbell tensed up and swung his right arm and hand toward Burke's head. It missed. Burke then grabbed Campbell with both arms and forced him to the ground. Burke handcuffed Campbell and as he stood him up, Campbell kicked Burke in the leg and attempted to spit in his face.

Burke put Campbell in his patrol car. Several people standing around the area clapped and said "thank you Mr. Stoney".

Burke made the trip to the County Jail where Ray Campbell was charged with Disorderly Intoxication and Resisting Arrest. Burke did not charge him with resisting arrest with violence, which is a felony. Campbell was drunk and the kick to Burke's leg did not hurt. A correctional officer told Campbell if you don't want to go to jail, just don't antagonize Sgt. Burke. Case closed by arrest.

"Wine is a mocker; strong drink is raging; whosoever is deceived thereby is not wise." Proverbs 20:1

CHAPTER 30

Currency Seized

On a Thursday afternoon, Sgt. Burke was patrolling the county. He had just departed the scene of a burglary of a residence, where two suspects were caught inside by Deputy Roe.

Lt. Maurice Taylor had stopped a 1983 blue Oldsmobile at approximately 3:30 p.m. He had observed this south bound vehicle swerve on Highway 103 and almost run another vehicle off the road. Taylor continued to follow the car another mile or so. During this time the vehicle again swerved across the center line almost causing an accident. Taylor stopped the car on Highway 103 just south of Muckville.

Sgt. Burke responded as a backup. Burke requested the K-9 team to also respond to Lt. Taylor's location. The stopped car was occupied by two males. Taylor and Burke asked the occupants to exit the car. As Lt. Taylor was writing the driver a citation, Deputy Davis and K-9 Apache arrived on the scene. The two men stated they were on the way to Miami, however, they were extremely nervous. Deputy Davis had K-9 Apache conduct a narcotic search around the exterior of the vehicle. Apache did not alert on the vehicle, but Burke had a suspicion that something was not right. He was usually on target when he got that feeling. So Burke asked for permission, from the two men, to search the car. Apparently the men were not too concerned about the possibility of the officers finding what was hidden inside the car. Burke searched the interior and hood area first. He found no contraband. Burke then opened the trunk which was completely empty. He noticed right away, however, that he was unable to observe the rear speakers which normally indicates a false wall has been constructed. Burke walked over and told Lt. Taylor there was a good chance that there was a secret compartment in the trunk. The officers then searched the two men for weapons, and handcuffed them for officer safety.

During the search of the trunk Burke noticed that the wall behind the back seat had been extended and there was new carpet throughout the entire trunk area. Burke had seen this on numerous occasions during traffic stops. Burke unfastened the car's rear seat back and pulled the seat out of the car. He then noticed a rectangular shaped hidden compartment in the center of the car body. The hidden compartment door was locked electronically. Burke was able to trace some wires from the hidden compartment to the front area of the car. Burke then located a toggle switch under the firewall near the radio. Burke turned the car keys to the on position and hit the toggle switch. He heard a noise from the back seat area that unlocked the latch to the door of the secret compartment. A search of the compartment revealed 21 large plastic bags full of money.

The two men said they had no knowledge of the money or who the car belonged to. Someone had paid them to drive the car to Miami and drop it off at a certain motel. Two days later they were to return to the motel, find the car, and drive it back to Georgia. Sgt. Burke had no way to prove the subject's knowledge of the money, or any criminal intent on their part, so they were released. Before the men left on foot, Lt. Taylor advised them the Sheriff's Office would be filing for court forfeiture of the car and money. They were also told they could come to the Sheriff's Office to claim the money, if they could prove how they got that much cash. However, if they made an appointment to get the money IRS also would be there at the Sheriff's Office. They would have to deal with the IRS Agents. They repeated, "it's not our money, and we don't know how it got there".

Burke transported the money to the Sheriff's Office. Lt. Taylor, Sgt. Burke, and Deputy Adams, counted the money. The total came to $445,344.

At Sheriff Rogers request, Sgt. Burke and Deputy Adams transported the money to a local bank to have it counted with a cash counting machine. The total at the bank again came to $445,344. The money was returned to the Sheriff's Office and placed in the evidence room, awaiting future forfeiture hearings.

During a later forfeiture hearing the car and money was given to the Tomahawk County Sheriff's Department. The Sheriff would use the money in future narcotic investigations and equipment. The Sheriff was pleased to receive this money. A great gift from the bad guys.

"Now thanks be to God for his gift, precious beyond telling his indescribable, inexpressible, free gift." 2 Corinthians 9:15

CHAPTER 31

Hidden Compartment in Gas Tank

On the afternoon of Wednesday, February 7th, Lt. Taylor and Sgt. Burke decided to go out on Highway 103 and stop a few vehicles for traffic violations. They also knew Highway 103 was a known drug corridor from Miami to all points north. Many people had been arrested on this highway for transporting marijuana and cocaine. Sgt. Burke asked Deputy Davis and K-9 Apache to stay in the immediate area of the town of Seminole. Burke and Taylor would be concentrating their efforts on Highway 103, one to four miles north of Seminole.

At 5:31 p.m. Lt. Maurice Taylor stopped a 1983 brown 4 door Chevy bearing a Georgia license plate on Highway 103, 2 miles north of Seminole, for speeding northbound. Burke was immediately there as a backup and asked the K-9 team to respond. The driver was found to be a 53-year-old retired female school teacher, later found to be Linda Jones from Miami Florida. The K-9 team arrived at the scene.

Lt. Taylor began writing a traffic citation to Jones who was standing by Taylor's patrol car. Deputy Davis had K-9 Apache conduct a narcotic search around the exterior of the stopped vehicle. Apache worked in a counter clockwise direction starting at the right front of the vehicle. Apache alerted to the rear end of the vehicle; the bumper area. Apache crawled up under the car and started scratching very aggressively at the rear of the gas tank. Davis then placed Apache in his patrol car after praising him for his alert. Davis told Jones that his K-9 was a certified narcotic detection dog and had alerted to her vehicle. Davis explained that her car would be searched for drugs. The officers searched the trunk and interior, but no drugs were located. Sgt. Burke crawled under the back end of the car to look for possible hidden compartments. Burke noticed the straps that hold the gas tank in place had been recently moved. Probably to remove the gas tank from the vehicle.

A wrecker was called to the scene and towed the car to a nearby gas station. The car was then put on a car lift so the officers could look underneath. At the gas station Burke observed unusual wires that had been sprayed with a new undercoating. Burke traced the wires under the firewall. Under the steering column of the interior of the car, he found a toggle switch. Burke had experience in tracing wires, for hidden compartments. Burke found a toggle switch at the end of the wires he had traced. Burke turned on the ignition switch, hit the toggle, and the back end of the gas tank dropped down. Inside half of the gas tank was 7 kilos of cocaine. Unknown persons had removed the gas tank and emptied the gas. They then made a triangular sized cut to the top of the tank, and removed the cut piece. This showed the entire interior of the tank. They then welded a piece of metal to divide the tank in half. They cut another piece to fit on the top, where the gasoline would be held. This way you could put gas on one side of the tank and have a concealed compartment on the other.

The gas tank had a solenoid switch to release the lock that would allow the rear of the tank to fall down while the front end was secured by hinges.

Burke removed the 7 kilos of cocaine from the tank. The tank was reattached in the locked position. The car was transported back to the original scene of the stop. Burke advised Lt. Taylor of the cocaine and he arrested Linda Jones for possession of cocaine and trafficking in cocaine.

Linda Jones stated she would cooperate with arresting officers, and help them find the suppliers and those receiving the drugs, if they would cut her a break. She was advised by Burke that he would let the State Attorney's office know she had cooperated with them, but the officers did not have the authority to make her any promises. Jones contacted her supplier and distributers stating her vehicle had broken down and she was at the Renegade Hotel in Seminole. Her vehicle was parked at the Renegade Hotel, by narcotic agents, and the cocaine was placed back in the secret compartment. Her car was disabled by pulling a wire to the distributor cap, and a microphone was placed in the rear bumper to capture any audible conversation around the vehicle. At this time a surveillance team, to include Lt. Taylor, Sgt. Burke, and two narcotic agents watched the vehicle from a van parked in the parking lot about 40 yards away. Other agents were inside several bottom floor motel rooms, to observe and film any action around the car. Jones was also in the room with female agents.

On Thursday, February 8, at approximately 1:30 p.m. two males arrived at the Renegade Hotel, from Miami, driving a newer model Cadillac. During the earlier phone conversation, they had agreed to pick up Jones to take her back to Miami. Shortly afterward two additional males arrived, driving a truck and pulling a trailer, to haul the broken down car to Valdosta, Ga. As they were attempting to start the car, the microphone picked up conversation where they were discussing the hidden cocaine in the gas tank. When the four males took possession of the disabled car containing the cocaine, officers from the surveillance van, and agents from the motel rooms, moved in and arrested them.

The four males and Jones were transported to the County Jail where they were all charged with Conspiracy to Traffic Cocaine, and placed on a $500,000 bond.

The truck, trailer, and Cadillac, were confiscated along with an additional $10,000 in cash. Case closed by arrest.

"A naughty person, a wicked man, walketh with a corrupt mouth." Proverbs 6:12

CHAPTER 32

Lost Child

It was an extremely cold winter afternoon with rain in the forecast. Deputy Roe received a call of a lost child, from the dispatcher. The mother of the female child called and stated her daughter had been playing in the back yard and was now missing. She advised the dispatcher she lived at 1313 Arrow Way, just north of Garnet.

At 5:05 p.m. Deputy Roe advised his dispatcher he was in route to the call. At 5:20 p.m. Deputy Roe arrived and obtained information of the lost child, and radioed the information to the other deputies and the dispatcher. The child was 6 years old, named Alaina Anderson. She had long blonde hair, blue eyes, and was last seen wearing jeans and a pink sweat shirt with white tennis shoes. The mother, Tammie Anderson, told Deputy Roe that Alaina had been playing in the back yard with her small brown and white beagle. She last observed Alaina approximately 45 minutes before she called the Sheriff's Office. Deputy Roe noticed the Anderson's lived on a cul-de-sac, and there was nothing but woods behind all the houses in that area.

Deputy Roe searched the back yard and walked in to the woods and searched a small area calling out for Alaina. Other neighbors who were advised of the situation were in the woods looking as well.

Deputy Roe asked Sgt. Burke to respond to the scene. Burke arrived at 5:49 p.m. By this time, it was starting to get dark. After briefly speaking to Deputy Roe, Burke called for Lt. Maurice Taylor and 3 other deputies to respond to the scene.

When Lt. Taylor and the other deputies arrived, Taylor took command. Lt. Taylor had a map of the area. He gave each deputy an area of the woods to search. There had been so many people wandering around the woods, Taylor did not believe a K-9 unit would be very useful.

Sgt. Burke and Deputies Roe, Adams, Earl, and Caruso started to search the woods. The mother, Tammie Anderson, stayed with Lt. Taylor in the Anderson's garage. It had gotten colder and started drizzling rain. By this time, Alaina had been missing over two hours. Lt. Taylor asked the dispatcher to have an ambulance respond to the scene in case it was needed. Taylor also called in several off duty deputies to assist in the search. Sheriff Lance Rogers had heard the call on his police radio at his residence. He responded to the scene as well.

The woods that surrounded the Anderson residence had lots of thick brush, along with holes, canals, and streams. There were a few small trails that ran through and around the area. The woods were a tough area to walk and search.

Burke was really worried about the small child, as he had 3 young boys himself, and could only imagine the agony and fear of one of them being missing. After completion of the search in the one area of the woods, Burke returned to the Anderson residence. He spoke briefly to the Sheriff and Lt. Taylor and had a quick cup of coffee. Burke then took off in a different area of the woods which had not been thoroughly searched.

About 30 minutes later, Burke came across the Anderson's Beagle. He started to feel hopeful. He believed Alaina might be close. Burke continued his search and after a total of approximately 3 hours had elapsed, Burke heard what he believed to be a faint call for help. Burke walked in the direction of the small voice. It was pouring rain by this time, and hard to hear anything but the rain, along with the thunder and lightning. Burke walked up on Alaina. She was lying on the ground, in the mud, crying. Burke immediately removed his jacket, wrapped her in it, and radioed back to Lt. Taylor that he had found the little girl. The mother, Tammie, started crying for joy. Burke advised Lt. Taylor he was about a mile to a mile and a half back in the woods and heading back toward the Anderson residence.

When Burke exited the woods, Tammie Anderson ran to hug Alaina. The little girl was wet, cold, shivering, and covered with mud. Burke handed Alaina over to EMT personnel who checked her out quickly and transported her to the hospital to be checked further. Alaina was checked out and released by the hospital, that evening. She was able to go home to her nice warm bed. Burke was extremely happy with the outcome. Lost child, found.

A few weeks later Sgt. Burke was asked by the Anderson's to stop by their residence. When Burke arrived, he received a big thank you and kiss from Alaina. She had helped her mother make cupcakes for Burke. Even though Burke was a big tough police officer, he found himself fighting back the lump in his throat. Burke gave Alaina a big hug.

"Rejoice always, pray without ceasing, give thanks in all circumstances; for this is the will of God in Jesus Christ for you." 1 Thessalonians 5:16-18

CHAPTER 33

Play Ball

Sgt. Stoney Burke had been involved with Law Enforcement Special Olympics for years. One year the department's S.W.A.T. team ran through the entire county carrying the torch to kick off the Olympics. They carried the torch they had received from the county north of them, ran it through Tomahawk County, and handed it off to the county south of them.

This year Burke planned to have some sort of fund raiser. They would donate all the money received to the Special Olympics.

Brain storm – Sgt. Burke's brother was a Gunnery Sergeant in the U.S. Marine Corp. He was a full time Marine, assigned at a U.S. Marine Reserve Unit in Central Florida. Stoney told his brother Gary Burke he had the idea of having a softball game to raise money. Law Enforcement vs. U.S. Marine Corp. Sgt. Gary Burke got permission from his commanding officer and Sgt. Stoney Burke got permission from the Sheriff. Game on! The game was scheduled for a Saturday, five weeks away. During this time, Stoney contacted all interested deputies and officers from several police departments in the county. Stoney also asked for and received lots of donations. The donations included hot dogs and buns, hamburgers and buns, drinks, cups, paper plates, napkins, chips, etc. Stoney was also able to get lots of volunteers to cook, work in the concession stand, and umpire the big game.

Stoney got his team out about twice a week to practice. He was sure the Marines were doing the same. Stoney also received a donation to purchase tee-shirts and caps for the law enforcement team.

Game day – It was a blistering summer afternoon. It started off by having a picture taken of the U.S. Marine Commander, Sheriff Rogers, several police chief's and the Burke brothers, Stoney and Gary. The hot dogs and hamburgers were cooking and filling the air with a great aroma.

After a brief warm up period for each team, the umpire yelled batter up, game time! The law enforcement team was the home team. Lots of people came to watch the game and ate lots of food, which was great for the fund raising part.

It was a hot and grueling game with temperatures that rose above 96 degrees. The teams went back and forth for several innings. The U.S. Marines then jumped on the law enforcement team, finally beating them 15-9. Stoney always contended that they didn't want to make the Marines look bad after they drove all that way to help them out. What great teams, and good sportsmanship.

After the game the fans and both teams had a great time eating together and just enjoying the moment for a good cause.

They raised lots of money for the Special Olympics. The law enforcement community appreciated all the donations and the U.S. Marines for their help.

Later on, Sgt. Stoney Burke sat down and wrote thank you letters to the U.S. Marines and all the local businesses that had donated items for the concession stand that was open during the game. The newspapers and local radio stations also helped by advertising the game. Again, thanks to all.

"Every good gift and every perfect gift is from above, coming down from the Father of lights with whom there is no variation or shadow due to change." James 1:17

CHAPTER 34

The Good, the Bad, and the Ugly

Sgt. Burke had spent many years in the career that he dearly loved; law enforcement. In every type of occupation there are bad apples. There is a gap between good and evil. Burke despised bad officers. The ones that push the limits, and especially the crooked officers. The officer's taking pay offs, officers stealing, officers physically abusing people, officers raping women, and officers using their badge for a crooked financial gain. The list could go on.

The Good

The majority of officers who dedicate their lives to community service are good, and out there for the right reasons; to protect, and serve. The good things that officers do is plentiful, but the news media rarely reports them. For instance, in the month of May, a mother and father were killed in a motorcycle accident. The investigating officer later had the task of telling the news to the 18-year-old son of the deceased parents. That son would be graduating from high school a week later. The officer told the young man he would be standing in his parents' place. The officer stated "I got your back".

The veteran officer kept good on his promise. When the son graduated and accepted his diploma, the officer waited for him at the end of the stage. There are stories like this each and every day that you will never hear.

The Bad

Sgt. Burke stopped a motorist one evening for unlawful speed. The motorist happened to be the father-in-law of a Captain from the Sheriff's Office. Burke issued the motorist a citation for unlawful speed. The citation was turned in to the Sheriff's Office at the end of Burke's shift. By Florida law, these citations have to be turned in to the Clerk of the County Court within a certain number of days.

Approximately 3 weeks later Sgt. Burke and Lt. Taylor were at the Sheriff's Office finishing some paperwork. Burke sat down at the Captain's desk. Several minutes later, Burke needed another pen. He opened the Captain's desk drawer to retrieve one. Inside the desk drawer was the citation he had written to the Captain's father-in-law. When the case came to court, it was dismissed due to the fact it had not been turned in to the Clerk's office in a timely manner. The citation should have never been in that desk. Burke or Taylor never said a thing about the citation, but all respect was lost for the Captain.

The Ugly

Sgt. Burke was assisting in the execution of a search warrant with many members of the Sheriff's Office. They were also assisted by the local police department. The search warrant was for illegal narcotics. One of the police officers was out front conducting security around the house in question, while the search was being conducted. The officer conducting security had made numerous narcotic arrests and had knowledge of other narcotic investigations and transactions. During the process of the search warrant, drugs, and U.S. Currency were confiscated. Also during the search, Sgt. Burke discovered a black ledger. As Burke and Lt. Taylor looked through the ledger they were shocked. The name of the police officer that was outside conducting security was written down in the ledger numerous times. Beside the officer's name it listed various amounts of money he had received. This was payment for information about police movements and investigations in order to protect the ongoing drug operation at that residence.

Burke and Lt. Taylor showed the ledger to the Chief Deputy of the Sheriff's Office and the officer in question's Chief of Police. This officer was soon relieved of his badge.

Above are just a handful of cases. In Burke's experience he found that 98% of law enforcement officers were good.

CHAPTER 35

Surprise Guest

It started out to be an extremely busy afternoon shift. Call after call, and numerous arrests by the deputies working under Sgt. Stoney Burke. At approximately 9:00 p.m. it had started to calm down. Sgt. Burke decided to try to stir up business. Burke parked his patrol car and advised the dispatcher he would be out on foot. He further advised the dispatcher he would be walking around in an area that was known to be crime ridden. This area had black, Mexican, Haitian, and Jamaican bars, all located in a very close proximity to each other. This makes for a huge breeding ground for turf wars, and cultural conflict. Burke walked about two blocks from his parked patrol car. He walked around some of the back alleys between the bars. There was usually lots of narcotic activity in this area.

While in the back alley, Burke decided to enter the back door of the big Harlem Bar. Burke was surprised that there was no lookout around the back door. Usually if an officer gets in the area, someone yells "police" or "fire in the hole" to warn everyone in the area. As Burke walked into the bar, he observed 6 to 8 males playing pool. Several others were sitting around tables, or casually walking around the bar. Burke walked up to a male sitting on a bench. He had a zip-lock baggie of marijuana sitting on the bench between his legs. The man was later identified as George Williams. Williams was rolling a joint (marijuana cigarette). Williams looked up and observed Sgt. Burke standing two feet in front of him. Burke grabbed the bag of marijuana and advised Williams he was under arrest. Burke quickly handcuffed Williams.

As Burke started to walk out the back door with his prisoner, trouble started. Burke and his prisoner were surrounded by 7 men; one with a knife. They stated, "you're not leaving here with him". Burke quickly stepped behind Williams, and wrapped his left arm around Williams' neck. The man with the knife started waving it in front of his face and smiled. He shouted at Burke "I'll cut you"! Burke was in fear of his safety at that time. Burke grabbed his service weapon with his right hand and immediately pointed it at the man wielding the knife. Burke told the men surrounding him "you don't want to do this guys". Burke then said "If anyone moves, I will kill 3 or 4 of you before you can get to me". Burke then had to say "which one of you feels lucky". The men backed up and Burke walked out the door with his prisoner. Burke called for another deputy to respond to the area. As he did not want to walk his prisoner two blocks to his patrol car.

Deputy Roe responded and took possession of Williams and transported him to the county jail. Burke then called for Deputy John Earl and told him to come to the bar. Burke waited in the back alley until Deputy Earl arrived. Burke told Earl to enter the front door of the bar, and Burke entered the back door. Once inside, Burke and Earl arrested the man who had pulled a knife on Sgt. Burke. This man was identified as Otis James. Burke and Earl walked James out of the front door, handcuffed him without incident, and he was placed in Deputy Earl's patrol car. Earl then dropped Burke off at his patrol car. Earl transported James to the County Jail.

At the County Jail, Burke charged George Williams with possession of marijuana, and Otis James with Assault with a Knife. Case closed by arrest.

Burke always believed in being a pro-active law enforcement officer; seeking out the bad guys before they had the opportunity to seek out innocent victims.

"Everyone who makes a practice of sinning also practices lawlessness; sin is lawlessness." 1 John 3:4

CHAPTER 36

Intoxicated Behavior

At 2:00 p.m., the Sheriff's Department dispatcher, Summer, broadcast a noise complaint to Deputy Celina Adams. The dispatcher stated a Wilma Hayes, who resides at 1515 CR 220, called in the complaint. Mrs. Hayes stated Harry Driggers was racing up and down the road in front of her house and spinning donuts. She was afraid that her elderly husband was going to get very upset and have a heart attack. Deputy Adams advised the dispatcher she would be in route to the Hayes residence. Mrs. Hayes lived about half a mile from Harry Driggers.

Sgt. Burke was only about a mile from the Hayes residence and told the dispatcher and Deputy Adams he was very close and he would handle the noise complaint. Burke also knew Harry Driggers. He was a drunk and Burke had arrested him several times for disorderly intoxication. Burke stopped by and talked to Wilma Hayes. She stated Driggers had been racing up and down the road in his truck with loud mufflers and spinning donuts in the grass. Burke told Mrs. Hayes he would take care of the situation. Burke left and drove to the Driggers residence.

Burke pulled into the Driggers' driveway. He noticed Driggers' truck was also parked in the driveway. As Burke approached the mobile home on foot, Driggers exited his house and stood on the open front porch. You had to walk up five steps to get up to the front porch. Harry stated "what the sam hill do you want"? Burke told Driggers there had been a complaint registered against him for racing up and down the road. Driggers had a beer in his right hand. He stated he did not care and Burke had not seen him driving. Burke then asked Mrs. Driggers and one of their sons, who had stepped out of the residence, not to let Driggers get behind the wheel and drive until he was sobered up.

Driggers then stated "you can kiss my butt, you s.o.b.". Driggers then pulled down his pants and underwear. He turned around, bent over, and shot Sgt. Burke a moon.

Driggers then stated "I'm going to get my gun and shoot you". He then turned and waddled into the open door, pants still around his ankles. Burke ran up the stairs after him. Driggers dove across the couch and grabbed a revolver sitting on the end table. Burke jumped on Driggers back and grabbed the gun also, with his left hand, and struck Driggers above his right eye with his fist. This caused a cut to Driggers eyebrow that started bleeding like a stuck pig. Burke took control of the gun and stuck it in his rear pocket. Driggers then started hitting and kicking at Burke. Both were standing up, and Burke grabbed Driggers and was attempting to get him outside the residence. During the struggle, they ended up on the front porch. Driggers still had his pants down around his ankles. Driggers tripped and both him and Burke fell down the flight of steps and hit the ground. When Burke hit the ground it knocked the wind out of him, however, he knew he still had to get control of Driggers. Both were covered with blood from Driggers busted eyebrow. Burke was wearing a white uniform shirt that was now mostly red. Burke was able to roll Driggers on his front side and handcuff him behind his back.

Deputy Adams had decided to head to the call anyway. She also knew harry Driggers. When she pulled into the driveway she got a surprise, and did not know what to think. She looked up and observed Burke lying on top of a naked man, which was face down, and blood all over both of them.

Deputy Adams jumped out of the car and ran toward the awkward situation on the ground. She realized Driggers had been handcuffed, and Burke was still trying to catch his breath. Deputy Adams got Driggers to his feet and his pants pulled up, and placed him in her patrol car. She looked back and Burke was getting up. Burke looked like he had been beaten bad. He was fine, however, because all the blood had come from Driggers. Deputy Adams then took photos of Burke and he left to go home to change uniforms. Deputy Adams transported Driggers to the hospital to get stitched up. She later transported him to the county jail.

Burke arrived at the County Jail and charged Driggers with Disorderly Intoxication, and Assault with a Firearm. Case closed by arrest.

"He drank of the wine and became drunk and lay uncovered in his tent." Genesis 9:21

CHAPTER 37

Battle with Bikers

It started out as a beautiful spring day, with a cool breeze. Sgt. Burke had a patrol supervisors meeting with the patrol commander at 9:30. After that meeting, Sheriff Rogers wanted Burke to attend one of the civic organizations lunches, and briefly discuss the ongoing drug trafficking problem that was coming through the county. Numerous vehicles were traveling through the county from South Florida to all points north. These vehicles were transporting large amounts of marijuana and cocaine.

At 1:10 p.m. Burke was finally free to patrol the county. He drove south and stopped at a friend's fish camp. Burke talked to his friend, Bill, about fishing. Burke had planned to go fishing on his next day off.

At 1:35 p.m. the dispatcher radioed a noise complaint to Deputy Ted Hicks about boys riding up and down the neighborhood roads on dirt bikes.

Burke was just leaving the fish camp and told the dispatcher he would take the call. He just happened to be about a mile away from Fisherman's Cove Road where the complaint was. Burke knew this road was a dead end. As Burke arrived in the area he observed 4 young boys, probably 13 to 15 years of age, driving up and down the road on their dirt bikes.

Burke stopped his patrol car and waved the boys over. The boys got off their bikes and approached Burke on foot. Burke had exited his patrol car and stood by the open driver's door. Burke did not remove his portable radio from its charger inside the car.

Burke explained to the boys, there had been a complaint and they could not operate the dirt bikes on the county roads. They needed to find a wooded area.

A man, later identified as Max Hill came walking over from a yard full of motorcycle bikers who were having a bar-b-que and drinking. Hill had a beer in his hand and told Burke to just leave the boys alone. They were not bothering anyone. Burke explained to Hill there had been complaints and as nicely as he could do it, told Hill it was none of his concern, and he should return to where he had come from. Hill's speech was slurred and he staggered as he walked. Burke knew the man was intoxicated. Hill stated "I'll make it my business". Burke again told Hill to leave, and he should not continue his behavior. Hill then stepped up and pushed Burke in the chest and stated, "leave the boys alone". Burke then told Hill he was under arrest, and forced Hill to the ground and was able to get one handcuff on him before another biker came running over and kicked Burke in the chest. Burke had no radio to call for help. Burke attempted to pull Hill closer to the patrol car to grab his radio. Burke was not going to let go of the other side of the handcuff. At this time several other bikers jumped in and started kicking Burke. Hill's wife ran over and was trying to give Hill some pills stating "he has a heart problem".

Meanwhile, a good neighbor saw what was happening and called the Sheriff's Office and stated "you better send help, the deputy out here is being beaten".

Burke had 4 bikers hitting and kicking him. Burke finally yelled at one of the boys standing at the side of his car, and ask him to pick up the radio microphone and say "Tomahawk 10, need help". The boy did as he was requested. Burke then kicked Hill between the legs. One man down. Burke let go of the handcuff at that time and was fighting with the other 4 bikers, and taking lots of punishment.

Within minutes, the cavalry arrived. Numerous patrol cars and unmarked detective cars came racing down the road to save Burke. When the officers arrived, Burke began to point out the different bikers that had attacked him, who by that time had started mingling with other bikers at the house to try to conceal their identity. Burke was able to pick out the ones that had assaulted him. He then grabbed Hill who was still on the ground and finished handcuffing him. He was placed in Burke's patrol car. The other bikers were loaded up in different patrol cars and hauled away to the county jail.

Investigators got statements from the boys, and the good Samaritan neighbor, about what had happened.

Burke then started transporting Hill to the county jail, when Hill began complaining it was hard for him to breathe. Burke radioed Lt. Taylor and told him of Hill's condition. Burke was advised to transport Hill to the hospital to get him checked out. Lt. Taylor also told Burke to get checked out himself, and he would send another deputy to watch Hill.

At the hospital Burke was checked out and received a handful of stitches here and there, after which he waited for Hill to be released. Hill was finally transported to the county jail by Burke. Burke charged Hill with Disorderly Intoxication, Battery on a Law Enforcement Officer, and Resisting Arrest with Violence. The other four bikers were charged with Battery on a Law Enforcement Officer. Case closed by arrest.

The next day on the front page of a local newspaper was a large picture of Hill and his wife. The caption read "heart patient brutally beaten by deputy". The Hill's later sued Burke and the Sheriff's Office.

Months later, Burke and the Sheriff's Office won the law suit. In the local paper, 6 pages back, there was a small paragraph telling of the results.

Burke was glad that all the bikers did not join in the fight that day!

"Let no corrupting talk come out of your mouths, but only such as is good for building up, as fits the occasion, that it may give grace to those who hear." Ephesians 4:29

CHAPTER 38

Armed Robbery in Progress

It was another sweltering hot day that started out extremely busy for Sgt. Stoney Burke's shift. First there was a domestic disturbance call that Burke responded to as a backup. Deputy John Earl arrested both the husband and wife. Sgt. Burke then responded to assist Deputy Celina Adams with a traffic accident with injuries. After leaving the scene of the accident, Sgt. Burke helped Deputy Bobby Caruso with a burglary of a residence. Deputy James Roe had received a suicide call. A man had shot himself in the head. Sgt. Burke spent time there until an investigator arrived to assist Deputy Roe. Burke was going from call to call, to assist his officers.

At 3:15 p.m. the Sheriff's dispatcher, Summer, sent out a radio call of a silent alarm, at a food store located on Highway 103, 2.5 miles south of the town of Garnet. This was a robbery alarm. Sgt. Burke advised the dispatcher he was just south of the store on Highway 103 and would be in route. Deputy Adams, who had completed her accident investigation, stated she would be in route from the north.

As Burke approached the food store he observed a young man running from the front door with a pistol in his right hand and a paper bag in his left hand. The man was wearing jeans, black tee shirt, and a red colored bandana covering his face. He ran to and jumped into the passenger seat of an awaiting black Chevy Camaro. The Camaro was backed up near the stores front door and driven by another young male wearing a dark colored tee shirt and white ball cap. The Camaro took off spinning and smoking it's tires in an attempt to leave the store parking lot, in a hurry. Burke radioed in the description of the getaway car and suspects to responding deputies.

Burke then decided he would speed up and ram the getaway Camaro. As the Camaro started to pull out onto the main road from the store parking lot, Burke rammed the Camaro. The front end of Burke's patrol car struck the driver's door area. The impact pushed the Camaro into a utility pole sitting on the corner. The passenger could not exit the car because his door was up against the pole. The driver could not get out either. Burke's patrol car had pushed in his door. Burke immediately jumped out with his 12-gauge shotgun loaded with buck shot. Burke pointed the shotgun toward the two occupants and ordered them to freeze. Both young men were holding pistols in their hands. There was a very tense moment. The men had pistols, but were looking down the business end of Burke's shotgun. By this time other deputies arrived as backup and surrounded the Camaro.

The driver later found to be Johnny Jones dropped his pistol out the window. The passenger later found to be Lonnie Jones remained armed.

Burke yelled at the passenger, Lonnie, to drop his gun or be shot. Lonnie sat there for several minutes weighing his options. He apparently decided it was not a good day to die. Lonnie dropped his gun. Burke walked closer to the Camaro and ordered the men to climb out the driver's door window and to lay face down on the ground. Burke held his shotgun on the two, while other deputies handcuffed them. Burke recovered both pistols and a brown paper bag containing $960 dollars which had been stolen from the food store.

The Jones', who were later found to be brothers, were transported to the county jail. Both were charged with Armed Robbery, Possession of a Firearm during the Commission of a Felony, and Grand Theft. Case closed by arrest.

Burke was extremely pleased with the outcome of the call. No one got hurt, the store got their money returned, and the two bad guys were arrested.

"The thief cometh not, but for to steal, and to kill, and to destroy. I am, that they might have life, and that they might have it more abundantly." John 10:10

CHAPTER 39

In the Heat of the Day

It was August and extremely hot with the temperatures reaching 100+ daily. Sgt. Burke was patrolling the county working the day shift. Burke decided to drive to the west side of the county. Burke drove into an area that had numerous canals and dirt roads near a local lake. This area was called Gator Trails.

Sgt. Burke was driving down one of the dirt roads and noticed a white van parked on one of the other roads, which ran parallel to the one he was on. Burke did not think much about the van at the time. Lots of people parked on these dirt roads and fished up and down the canals leading from the lake. Burke left the area and continued patrolling the county.

Burke then proceeded to the county courthouse. He had traffic court on 3 separate traffic tickets he had issued a month earlier.

Burke was off duty the next two days. He did what he loved to do. He went fishing and did lots of honey dos around the house. Burke also invited his shift over for a bar-b-que supper. Burke loved to cook, and enjoyed the leisure time with his officers and their families.

Burke returned to work on Tuesday morning to work his last week of day shifts. His squad would be rotating to the afternoon shift, which was Burke's favorite.

The morning was slow, and Burke and Lt. Maurice Taylor met for lunch to discuss some shift business. They had lunch at the Swamp Diner. They ate gator tail. Burke was a die-hard Seminole fan. He did not like a thing about gators, except when he had the opportunity to eat them.

After lunch Burke decided to again drive to the west side of the county. He was going to check out the area of Gator Trails which contained the canals and many dirt roads. He wanted to see if anyone was fishing. He really wanted to know if they were catching fish.

As Burke arrived in the area, he observed the same white van he had seen parked there three days before. Burke believed the van was parked in the same spot. Burke said to himself, this is not good.

Burke parked about 30 yards in front of the van. He observed the driver's window was rolled down, and he could not see anyone up or down the canals.

As Burke approached the van on foot he could hear the swarming of lots of flies and then the stench of death hit his nostrils. Burke then observed hundreds of flies around the van. Burke knew this was going to be a bad day. There was no one in the driver or passenger seats. Burke did notice a folded up piece of paper and a wallet sitting on the driver's seat.

Burke walked around the van and opened the side sliding door, and again the stench of decaying flesh slapped him in the face. Burke backed up, bent over, gagging and puking.

Burke then observed a dead man sitting in the back seat. He was bloated, with maggots all over him. Burke called on his radio to the Sheriff's Department, and requested investigators to respond to a possible suicide. Burke opened all the van's doors and windows to help air it out a little. Within 45 minutes, two investigators and the county coroner arrived.

On the van's front seat, the investigators found a man's wallet and a suicide note. The name on the driver's license was John Doe. The suicide note was dated 6 days earlier. This meant John Doe had probably been deceased for 6 days, in the heat of the summer inside a closed van. The note also had the name of his next of kin, and a phone number.

From past experience, Burke knew it would help to put cigarette filters in his nose covered with Vicks vapor rub. This would help a little to mask the odor. Burke also called for a wrecker to respond to the scene.

Burke assisted the coroner and the investigators in removing John Doe from the van very slowly, and placing him in a body bag. The slow movement was necessary to prevent the bloated body from bursting and spewing body fluids.

Investigators searched the van and recovered a .357 magnum revolver on the floor board in a puddle of body fluid which had leaked out of John Doe, down the seat, and on to the floor board.

The coroner transported the body to the morgue for a full autopsy. Burke waited for the investigators to finish the initial investigation and for the wrecker to leave with the van.

Burke had seen numerous suicides in his career. But this one was bad, because of the length of time the body had been in the closed hot van, during the heat of the summer.

Burke then had to go notify Jane Doe, the daughter of the deceased, of her father's death. Jane stated her mother had died two years earlier. She further explained that her father had cancer. He had been going through chemo and radiation and had been in lots of pain for years. Jane stated that she was not surprised of what her father had done. Case closed by suicide.

"Be not over much wicked, neither be you, foolish; why should you die before your time." Ecclesiastes 7:17

CHAPTER 40

Gun Case Cocaine

Sgt. Stoney Burke began the squads first day on the afternoon shift by starting the monthly patrol vehicle inspections for each of his deputies. He conducted two inspections, then headed to the north end of the county. While in route to the north end Burke observed and stopped a red 1991 Dodge Spirit, after it weaved from the right lane into the emergency lane three times. Burke advised the dispatcher of the traffic stop and gave her the location of the stop, and the Florida tag number on the vehicle. The vehicle was occupied by two males.

The Dodge had been rented by the driver, Berry Angelo, from Miami. The passenger was Herbert Lewis, also from Miami. The vehicle had been rented from Don's Rent-a-Car in South Florida.

Burke observed the men were extremely nervous and had conflicting stories about their travel plans. Burke then asked the K-9 team to respond to his location on Highway 103, three miles north of Seminole. Several minutes later, Deputy

Ethan Davis and K-9 Apache arrived on the scene. Burke had the driver and passenger get out of the car. Burke asked Deputy Davis to have K-9 Apache conduct a narcotic search of the vehicle. Burke then began to write Berry Angelo a traffic citation for Failure to Drive within a Single Lane.

Deputy Davis got Apache out of his patrol car and walked him to the front end of the stopped vehicle. Davis gave Apache the command, find the dope. Apache started walking around the car in a counter clockwise direction, sniffing the exterior of the vehicle as he walked. When Apache reached the rear of the vehicle he got aggressive and started scratching and biting at the seam around the trunk lid. That was Apache's alert for narcotics. Deputy Davis then praised Apache and placed him back into his patrol car. Deputy Davis told the two occupants that Apache was a certified narcotic detection dog and that he had alerted to their vehicle. The two were told that their vehicle was going to be searched. Lt. Maurice Taylor arrived and stood watching the two suspects. Burke started searching the interior of the car. He found no narcotics but found one revolver under each seat. Burke then asked the driver for the keys to the trunk. Both men stated they did not have a trunk key and had never been in the trunk.

Burke then removed the back seat and gained entry into the trunk. Inside the trunk Burke found a locked gun case. The gun case was forced open. Inside, Burke found a SPAS 9 shot .12-gauge assault shotgun. Burke said to himself, now that's a tough gun. Underneath the shotgun was a large yellow plastic bag. Inside the bag Burke discovered large slabs of crack cocaine. Burke conducted a narcotic presumptive test on the suspected crack cocaine and it came back positive. Burke then weighed the cocaine and found it to be 2 pounds.

The car was towed to the Sheriff's Office impound lot. Sgt. Burke transported the two men to the county jail. Both Berry Angelo and Herbert Lewis were charged with Trafficking in Cocaine over 400 grams, and Possession of a Firearm in the Commission of a Felony. Bond was set at $500,000 for each subject. Case cleared by arrest.

"There is no peace, says the Lord, for the wicked." Isaiah 57:21

CHAPTER 41

Was I a Good Cop?

Over the years I have been asked several times if I was a good cop. I hope I can answer that question at the end of this short chapter.

It's been 42 years since I first put on a law enforcement uniform, in November of 1974. And now it's been numerous years since I've retired.

I have looked back over my chosen career. As you know there is good and evil, right and wrong. I always tried to do good, and right. I chose this career, mainly because I looked up to my father, Ron Stanley. Dad spent 41 years as an officer in the State of Florida.

I was a very street smart officer. I was always extremely aware of my surroundings and looking and thinking ahead. This was a great blessing to me. I found myself at the right place, at the right time, more often than not. However, there were times I was in the wrong place at the wrong time. I paid my dues during these times. I was hurt on several occasions during my career. One night I was struck in the face with a lead pipe. On the way to the hospital in the air flight helicopter, I asked God to come into my life and asked him to forgive me of all my sins.

I spent many years as an FTO (field training officer). I trained many young officers; some still working, and many retired. I have been told by numerous officers that I trained "thank you, if it were not for you I would have never stayed in law enforcement." Or "because of you, you made me a better officer". This kind of makes me feel good to be told I actually made a difference.

Like most cops, I had to uphold that tough guy image. I've been there and done that. But on the other hand I've also cried like a baby on several occasions. When you see a baby or a small child hurt or killed. When you have to go to a home late at night and tell parents that their teenage son or daughter has been killed in a traffic accident, etc. It makes a tough guy weak at the knees.

I have gone out of my way many times to avoid arresting someone. I would take an intoxicated person home, call a cab, or call a parent, instead of arresting their child for some small crime, or being drunk. An act of kindness instead of ruining a person's life just to make another arrests. Believe me, I have made hundreds of arrests in my career.

During my career I worked for several agencies where I usually climbed in rank, quickly. I would have to say after sitting back and looking at my career in law enforcement,

I made some good choices and some not so good. I always believed in being honest, fair, and courteous to all people.

I believe in my heart, yes, I was a good officer.

I respect all the men and women that wear the badge of honor; the past, the present, and the future officers. Please don't tarnish it.

God bless you, my brothers and sisters.

About the Author

Jon Eston Stanley was born in Brooksville, FL on November 7, 1951. During his early childhood years, he grew up in Dade City, Pasco County, FL. Jon's father, Ronald Stanley, worked with the Pasco County Sheriff's Office, and as the Assistant Chief of Police of the Dade City Police Department.

In October, 1964, Jon moved to Gainesville, FL with his family, when his father accepted a job with the Alachua County Sheriff's Office as the head investigator in charge of the Criminal Investigation Division. Jon attended and graduated from Gainesville High School in June of 1970.

In January of 1971 Jon joined the U.S. Army and became a paratrooper serving in both the 82nd and 101st Airborne Divisions.

Jon began his law enforcement career on November 7, 1974 as a Deputy Sheriff with the Palm Beach County Sheriff's Department, located in West Palm Beach, FL. When hired, Jon worked under Sheriff William Heidtman, and later, Sheriff Richard Willie.

During the next 20+ years, Jon worked for several other agencies to include the Sumter County Sheriff's Department in Bushnell, Florida. Jon worked in various positions. He served as patrol officer, patrol supervisor, investigator, investigation division supervisor, narcotics, K-9 officer, field training officer, S.W.A.T. member, motorcycle officer, part time marine patrol officer, and worked in a highway drug interdiction unit. Jon also worked in and for several multi-county agency drug task forces being dual deputized by several different Florida Sheriff's. He worked as a drill instructor at a juvenile boot camp, and as a Chief of Police.

Jon was a certified police instructor and K-9 instructor teaching through the Withlacoochee Vocational Technical Center in Inverness, FL. Jon attended the 680-hour course in basic K-9 training and the 320-hour course in K-9 Narcotic Detection at the St. Petersburg Police Department's K-9 training school. Jon also attended basic and advanced SWAT Schools.

Jon attended Santa Fe Junior College, Palm Beach Junior College, Lake-Sumter Community College, and St. Leo College. Jon also has more than 3000 hours in police related schools, seminars, and classes, not including his college courses. Jon has attended the U.S. Department of Justice Drug Enforcement Administration (DEA) narcotic school, and the FBI hostage negotiation class. He has attended several classes at the Institute of Police Traffic Management (IPTM) located at the University of North Florida, Jacksonville, FL where he became a certified radar instructor.

Jon was a member of the Florida Police Chief's Association, the Florida Narcotics Officer Association, and the United States Police K-9 Association. He has received numerous citations and awards during his career, to include Silver Star for Bravery from the American Law Enforcement Officers Association. He also received an Outstanding Commendation Award from the American Police Hall of Fame.

"Even though I walk through the valley of the shadow of death, I will fear no evil." Psalm 23:4

"May God himself, the God of peace, sanctify you through and through. May your whole spirit, soul and body, be kept blameless at the coming of our Lord Jesus Christ. The one who calls you is faithful and he will do it." 1 Thessalonians 5:23-24

Index

Special Thanks

➢ God, My Heavenly Father – For being patient with me, and leading me in the right direction. And blessing me with a wonderful wife and family.

➢ Steven Hopkins, Hopkins Printing Inc., Dothan, AL hopkinsprinting@hotmail.com - Book Cover Design

➢ Colleen Stanley (my wife) – Typing, editing, and all the labor associated with bringing my thoughts together in a book.